MACPHERSON'S CARAVAN

'S-Stolen g-goods!' stammered Macpherson, staring at the parcel. 'I never saw it before. I don't know how it got into the caravan.'

To be arrested for possessing stolen goods was the last thing Macpherson expected as Slow-Coach the piebald pony plodded towards the Scotland–England border. England – a foreign country! But before he knew what was happening the young messenger boy was whisked away in a police car, leaving Grandpa and Maisie Murphy bewildered on a lonely Scottish road.

Of course, the unexpected is always happening to Macpherson, and this holiday in a real gypsy caravan is no exception. Cheerful and eternally optimistic, he and his two companions rattle and creak from one extraordinary adventure to another . . .

Cover illustration by Val Biro

ABOUT THE AUTHOR

Lavinia Derwent was born in No-Man's-Land on a farm on the Scottish side of the Border, so remote that she knew more animals than human-beings. Her head being full of 'beasts', she made up stories about them, invented a character called TAMMY TROOT and later an island called SULA, full of seals and sea-birds.

When she came to live in the big city of Glasgow she met many human-beings, but none that interested her more than a cheerful boy whom she saw in the street, lugging a heavy message-basket. MACPHERSON! Since then Macpherson has taken the place of 'beasts' in her head. Through him she has had many exciting adventures; and is delighted that so many children also follow his fortunes, sending her letters and drawings about Macpherson, Maisie and other characters.

Lavinia Derwent has written many children's books. But of all her many characters she has the softest spot for MACPHERSON.

Macpherson's Caravan

Lavinia Derwent

Illustrated by Lesley Smith

KNIGHT BOOKS
Hodder and Stoughton

Text copyright © 1968 Lavinia Derwent
Illustrations © 1979 Lesley Smith

First Published by Burke publishing

This edition first published in 1979 by Blackie &
Son Limited

Knight Books edition 1981

British Library C.I.P.

Derwent, Lavinia
  Macpherson's caravan.
  I. Title.
  823'.914[F]   PR6007.E642M/

  ISBN 0–340–26527–2

Printed and bound in Great Britain for
Hodder and Stoughton Paperbacks, a
division of Hodder and Stoughton Ltd.,
Mill Road, Dunton Green, Sevenoaks,
Kent (Editorial Office: 47 Bedford
Square, London, WC1 3DP) by
Richard Clay (The Chaucer Press) Ltd.,
Bungay, Suffolk

By the same author:

Macpherson's Lighthouse Adventure
Macpherson's Skyscraper
Macpherson's Island

Contents

I

Caught by the Police

It was a real gypsy caravan, drawn by a piebald pony, and driven by the King of the Gypsies himself.

He looked very young—only a boy—and very shabby to be a king. His knees were bare. His green jersey was out at the elbow. He had no crown on his ruffled hair. Yet he held himself as proudly as if he was driving in a golden carriage.

"Gee-up, Slow-Coach! Look lively!"

The piebald pony blew down his nose and plodded on at his own speed. Slow-Coach had never looked lively in his life. Not that there was any need to hurry. They were far away from the city on a quiet country road. Not a soul in sight. Not a sound to be heard. Not a care in the world.

Suddenly, the King of the Gypsies sat up and stared at a notice straight ahead. He had reached the frontier. Another few steps and he would be in a strange country.

SCOTLAND—ENGLAND. He whirled round in his seat and called out: "Hooray! We've reached the Border! Hurry up, Grandpa! We'll soon be in England. *Grand-pa!*"

It was, of course, Macpherson the message-boy who was driving the piebald pony. *He* was King of the Gypsies, and many other things besides; but only in his imagination. A wealthy Sheikh, for example, with slaves at his command; and Superman, Star of Outer Space. He had only to clap his hands, and one of his servants would appear.

"What is thy wish, O Master?"

"I wish thee to make Grandpa hurry up so that we can cross over the Border together."

It was not easy to make the old man hurry up. He had got down from the caravan to stretch his legs and lighten Slow-Coach's load. The pony was slow, but Grandpa was slower. He had fallen far behind, not only because of his shaky legs. Someone—a small girl—was tugging at his hand and asking excited questions.

"Oh, look! There'th another flower. What'th it called?"

"That's a wild rose," said Grandpa, peering at the hedgerow.

"Tho it ith! Can I pull it?"

Wee Maisie Murphy could not get over the fact that wild flowers were free. What was more, they were real, not made of paper or plastic. She, too, had jumped down from the caravan and was dancing from one side of the road to the other, wanting to pick every free flower in sight. But as soon as she heard her hero calling, all else was forgotten.

"Come on!" She tried to pull Grandpa along. "Macpherthon wantth uth to hurry up."

Macpherson had stopped the caravan and was waiting for them. Letting the reins fall from his hands, he took a breath of fresh hill air. This was the life! So still; so peaceful! Nothing to be seen except a skylark skimming overhead. Nothing to be heard except the bleating of a sheep.

Suddenly, everything changed. The air was filled with harsh noises. The pony raised his head and began to snort in protest. From the English side of the Border a police car came roaring up the road. The screech of its siren could be heard for miles. From the Scottish side another policeman on a motor-cycle came zig-zagging past Grandpa and Maisie and drove straight towards the caravan. Macpherson was hemmed in on both sides.

"What's up?" he asked, in a daze.

The policemen had met and were talking rapidly to each other in low tones. Then one of them called out to Macpherson: "Come down from that caravan, young fella, and you'll soon find what's up. We want to see what you've got in the back."

Macpherson scrambled down, protesting, "There's nothing there that shouldn't be there. You can look, if you like."

"We'll look all right!" said one of the men, pulling back the flap.

Macpherson waited at the side of the road, feeling nervous, though he had nothing to be guilty about. There was only an old tent inside, some sleeping-bags, a cooking-stove, a few pots and pans. . . .

"Got it! Here it is!"

The English policeman gave a shout of triumph, and pounced on an untidy parcel tied up in newspaper. It had been lying at the back of the caravan, tucked under a waterproof sheet.

"That's it! Stolen goods! Now then, young fella, what have you got to say for yourself?"

"S-Stolen g-goods!" stammered Macpherson, staring at the parcel. "I never saw it before. I don't know how it got into the caravan."

"So you say! Come along! We'll sort it all out at the police station. Get into the car!"

"No, no! I don't want to come! I'm not guilty! Grandpa! Come and help . . . !"

But Grandpa was too far off to reach him in time.

Meet Mr Grim

It had all started weeks before on a pouring wet day in the big city of Glasgow.

Macpherson was running along the street with the rain splashing on his bare legs. Not that he noticed it. He was too busy breaking the world's speed-record. He could hear the crowd cheering him on at the Olympic Games.

"Come away, Macpherson! A gold medal for Macpherson, the fastest runner in the world!"

Macpherson had a good reason for running. He had to reach Old Skinflint's shop in time. He knew only too well what would happen if he was late. Old Skinflint (whose real name was Mr McGlashan, the grocer) would be looking at his watch, counting the minutes as if they were money.

"Late again! I'll skin him alive! Message-boys! They're perfect pests! I'll take him by the scruff of the neck...."

Macpherson skidded through the open door

and put on his brakes so suddenly that he almost fell over backwards. Then his eyes opened wide with surprise. There was no one in the shop except Miss Peacock, the plump, pleasant assistant. Not a sign of Old Skinflint.

"Mercy me! Is *he* late?"

Macpherson could not have been more amazed if the sky had fallen down.

"No," said Miss Peacock, solemnly. "He's not coming."

"Not coming!" said Macpherson, in a daze. "What's up?"

"He's in hospital. With appendicitis."

"What?" Macpherson could not believe his ears. Imagine the grocer being ill! Imagine him having an appendix, like everyone else! It put a different light on Old Skinflint. He became almost a human being.

"Is he very ill?" Macpherson asked.

"Ill enough," said Miss Peacock. "He's going to have an operation this morning."

"Mercy me!" Old Skinflint was becoming more human every moment. "Is there anything we can do?" Macpherson looked at the empty space behind the counter. He would sooner have had the grocer raging at him than think of him lying ill in hospital.

"We'll just have to get on with the job," said

Miss Peacock, beginning to look brisk. "His cousin's coming to take charge."

"Goodness!" So Old Skinflint had a cousin as well as an appendix! "Is it a he or a she?"

"It's a he. His name's Grim."

"Away!" Macpherson's heart sank. "That's a terrible name."

But he was not a terrible man. They knew the moment he came through the door that Mr Grim did not suit his name. The very opposite! He was a round, tubby man with a bright red face full of smiles.

"A fine day for the ducks," he grinned, shaking the rain from his hat. "So this is Old Tight-Fist's place."

"We call him Old Skinflint ..." began Macpherson before Miss Peacock could stop him; but Mr Grim only chuckled.

"A very good name for him, too! Never did see eye-to-eye with me cousin. All the same, when someone's in trouble, we've got to spring to it. Who's the boss here? You?"

He looked at Macpherson, who took a step back and said: "Me? Oh no, Mr Grim, sir. I'm only the message-boy."

"And what's wrong with that? I've been a message-boy in me day. Been lots of other things as well. Been a cowboy, and a clown, and an ostrich-farmer...."

There was no end to what Mr Grim had been. All the time he was talking, he was beaming at Miss Peacock, tying one of Old Skinflint's white aprons round his tubby waist, and getting ready for action behind the counter.

"You'll have to keep me right, me dear," he told Miss Peacock. "Don't know a thing about prices. Can't even count, if it comes to that! But if you keep an eye on me, me dear, we'll get along all right."

They got along like a house on fire. It was amazing what a different feeling there was in the shop without Old Skinflint watching them like a hawk. Never had the time flown past so quickly. Mr Grim had so many strange adventures to relate and was always in such good humour. He chatted to all the customers as if they were old friends. They were pleased to have such a warm welcome when they came into the shop, and to be served by someone who did not worry about overweight.

Unlike his cousin, Mr Grim did not hold with scrimping and saving.

"Better to give more than less!" said he, handing out lavish helpings of sugar and butter and tea and biscuits. It was as well Old

Skinflint could not see him. The grocer's
temperature would have shot up to the sky.

With such an easy-going master to please,
Macpherson worked harder than ever before.
The rain did not seem so wet nor the message-
basket so heavy when he knew there would be
a word of praise for him at the end of the day.

"Back already! Well done, me boy! You
must have wings! Let's have a cup of tea."

Mr Grim was a great one for his cups of tea. "Old Skinflint would have a fit," thought Macpherson, as he sat in the back-shop, drinking the hot sweet brew and eating a chocolate biscuit. It was the best kind, with silver-paper wrapped round it.

"Have another," said Mr Grim, thrusting it into the boy's hand. "Did I tell you about the time I joined the Foreign Legion?"

Mr Grim had done everything and been everywhere. India! China! Africa! Japan! He had just come back from the South Sea Islands to have a short holiday at home before going off again to the ends of the earth. Even on his holiday he had wanted to be on the move.

"Bought meself an old caravan, for a jaunt round Britain," he told Macpherson.

"Goodness!" Macpherson looked at him enviously. "A real caravan?"

Mr Grim nodded. "Sure! A real gypsy one, with a piebald pony. I would be off in it right now if me cousin hadn't turned ill."

Miss Peacock jumped to her feet. "That reminds me. I'd better ring the hospital to find out how he is."

"You do that, Miss Peacock, me dear. Pass the tea-pot, Macpherson."

Macpherson had a sudden guilty feeling as

he sat on an upturned tea-chest, sipping his second cup. He had forgotten all about Old Skinflint—and him suffering in hospital. With such a lively companion as Mr Grim, it was easy to forget everything else. He had almost forgotten Grandpa and what was happening at home. But now it was Mr Grim himself who reminded him.

"Tell me about yourself, Macpherson, me boy. Where do you live? Hold on! Let me guess! I know! Buckingham Palace!"

"Away!" said Macpherson, shaking his head. "I live at Number Five, Clyde-View Tenements."

"There's an address for you! Go on, me boy. Tell me all about it."

There seemed little to tell, after Mr Grim's adventures, but Macpherson did his best. He told about Grandpa making ships-in-bottles. He told about Aunt Janet working so hard to make ends meet. He told about wee Maisie Murphy and all the neighbours. Then he let his imagination run riot.

"Of course, when I'm a millionaire I'm going round the world. Like you, Mr Grim, sir. I'll take Grandpa with me. He could do with a change of air...."

Just then Miss Peacock came back and said,

"He's through!"

Macpherson went white. "You mean, he's ...?"

"No, no; he's fine! He's through his operation. As well as can be expected."

Macpherson gave a sigh of relief. It was strange how you could alter your feelings for someone when he was ill. "Maybe we could send him something," he suggested.

"Flowers?" said Miss Peacock doubtfully. Somehow flowers and Old Skinflint did not go together.

Mr Grim chuckled. "If I know me cousin, he'd sooner see his account-books." He pulled out a handful of coins from his pocket. "Away you go, Macpherson, me boy, and buy a Get Well card. Keep the change and get something for your Grandpa. I like the sound of the old gentleman."

"Oh, thanks, Mr Grim, sir. Yes, I will."

Macpherson was off like a shot. He bought the biggest and best Get Well card he could find. A funny one, with an elephant on it, wearing boxing-gloves, no less! Underneath were the words: HOPE YOU WILL SOON BE FIGHTING FIT. Macpherson was not sure if Old Skinflint would see the point, but maybe it would cheer him up a bit.

There was plenty of change left over, enough to buy some of Grandpa's favourite tobacco, as well as some peppermints for Aunt Janet and a lollipop for Maisie. Even so, there was still fivepence left.

Macpherson handed it over when he came back to the shop. "Here you are, Mr Grim, sir; and thanks very much. You're awful kind."

"Keep it, me boy," beamed Mr Grim. "It'll do to start you off on your travels."

"What travels?" said Macpherson, looking at him in surprise.

"I thought you were going round the world!" Mr Grim winked at Miss Peacock who tried to wink back, but she was not very good at it. Had they been plotting something, these two? "You might even go off in me caravan some day," went on Mr Grim, as if the thought had just struck him. "Might as well make use of it."

"Goodness gracious!"

"Why not?" continued Mr Grim. "You'll be working extra hard while me cousin's off. When he comes back. I might persuade him to let you have a holiday."

Of course, it was only an idea, but such a wonderful idea that Macpherson almost stood on his head every time he thought of it. King of the Gypsies, driving his own caravan, with Grandpa by his side! What could be better?

He worked harder than ever. He ran with his message-basket so that he could get back sooner to the shop. He offered to do extra jobs.

"Leave it to me, Mr Grim, sir, I'll sweep out the shop."

"Don't bother yourself, Miss Peacock. I'll dust the counter for you."

He was ready and willing to come early and stay late. Not once did he break an egg or drop any apples out of the message-basket. Even Old Skinflint would have had to admit that Macpherson was doing his best.

Macpherson had almost forgotten the grocer till one day he found himself opposite the hospital gates.

"Maybe I should go in and visit him, poor soul!"

Macpherson stood there, tussling with himself. He would sooner have gone straight back to the shop. He would miss his tea and chocolate biscuit. But what did that matter for once? The trouble was, if you went to visit someone in hospital, you had to take something with you. A wee present.

Macpherson felt in his pocket. He had only

fivepence there—the fivepence that was to start him on his journey round the world.

"Och well, it's in a good cause," he sighed, taking out the money. He saw himself as Macpherson the Martyr, giving up all his worldly wealth for the sake of someone who was not worth it. In another moment he would be St Macpherson with a halo round his head.

Then he remembered Grandpa's wise advice. "If you're going to do anything for anybody, Macpherson, do it willingly, and stop thinking about yourself."

"Right!" said Macpherson, squaring his shoulders. He went up to the old flower-woman who sat at the gates. "Have you anything for fivepence, please?"

It was nearing the end of the day, and she was anxious to get rid of the few flowers left.

"Here's a wee bunch of violets, son. They'll cheer somebody up."

Macpherson put the bunch of violets in his empty message-basket and made his way into the hospital. He had to be careful not to slip on the floors. Everything was so well-polished, and there was a strange, sharp smell in the air. He began to feel a little faint, as if *he* was going through an operation. But he pulled himself together when he reached the men's ward.

It was strange to see the gaunt figure of Old Skinflint sitting up in bed wearing red-and-white striped pyjamas. Macpherson did not notice him at first. What attracted his attention was the Get Well card propped up on the locker beside the patient's bed. It was the only one there, and Old Skinflint was peering at the elephant over his spectacles.

When Macpherson came forward the grocer peered at him instead.

"What are *you* doing here?" he asked in his usual gruff voice.

"I—I've come to see you, Mr McGlashan, sir."

"Huh! Have you delivered all the groceries?"

"Yes, I have, Mr McGlashan, sir."

Old Skinflint shot him a glance of suspicion. "You haven't shoogled any eggs?"

"No, sir; no, I haven't."

They might have been in the shop instead of in the hospital. Until Macpherson remembered the violets.

"Here's a wee bunch of flowers," he said, laying them on the bed.

"Tuts! Waste of money!"

All the same, Old Skinflint picked them up and took a sniff at them. Then he laid them down and gave Macpherson a strange look. He muttered something which Macpherson took to be "Thank you"—though it was a bit too much to expect from a man like Mr McGlashan. To fill in an awkward pause, Macpherson asked him how he was feeling.

"Fine," grunted the grocer. "I'll soon be out of here. How's that cousin of mine getting on in the shop? He hasn't lost any customers, I hope?"

"Oh no, Mr McGlashan, sir. He's got some new ones."

"Huh! Wait till I see what a mess the books are in."

"They're okay! Miss Peacock's keeping an eye on them."

Old Skinflint dropped the violets and gave Macpherson one of his sternest looks. "Well, I'll soon be back to keep an eye on you all."

It sounded like a threat, and it brought the conversation to a standstill. Macpherson shuffled his feet on the polished floor and said uneasily, "I'd better be getting back to the shop."

"Yes, you'd better! No use hanging about here." He glared at Macpherson; yet when he said goodbye his voice was not quite as gruff as usual. "Off you go, now! Goodbye, Macpherson."

Macpherson skidded across the floor and turned at the door to wave. He got no wave back. But his heart warmed when he saw that Old Skinflint had picked up the violets and was holding them up to his nose. Maybe he was human, after all.

Macpherson sped back to the shop, not sure whether his visit had been a success or not. As for going round the world, he could always get there by magic.

"Slave!"

"I am here! What is thy command, O Master?"

"I command thee to soften Old Skinflint's heart and let me go off in the caravan."

"Your wish is my command. It shall be done!"

Having issued his orders, the King of the Gypsies put the empty message-basket on his head to keep out the rain, and ran back to the grocer's shop.

3

On the Road

"Oh Macpherthon! Ithn't it great?"

"It's not bad."

Not bad! Wee Maisie Murphy was having the time of her life. So was Macpherson, judging by the look on his face. But it would not do to agree with everything Maisie said. After all, she was only a lassie and had to be kept in her place.

"Ho-ro! Up she rises!" sang out Grandpa. He was more used to ships than caravans. Yet he had not taken long to get the hang of driving the placid pony. "It'll soon be your turn, Macpherson. Wait till we get off the main road. Ship ahoy, Slow-Coach! Straight ahead!"

Slow-Coach plodded on, with the caravan rattling and creaking behind him. The car drivers turned their heads as they flashed past, and looked amused. They were used to seeing smart up-to-date caravans on the roads, nothing as broken-down and old-fashioned as this.

They were all new and shiny, like little houses on wheels, drawn by powerful motor cars, not by a snorting pony.

The people seemed amused, too, at the three figures sitting up in front. In the middle, holding the reins, was an old man with a straggling beard. He wore a sailor's jersey, and had an old oilskin hat perched on his head. The boy at his right side could scarcely keep still for excitement. He was bouncing up and down in his seat, itching to get his hands on the reins.

The small girl on the other side already had her hands full. She was hugging a snow-white kitten to her heart, and talking to it as if it were a baby. "Go to thleep, you!"

Of course, it was the cheerful Mr Grim who had worked the miracle. Macpherson never knew what he had done to soften Old Skinflint's heart. The main thing was, he was free from the shop, with a caravan at his command.

Mr Grim had been to the Tenements to talk it over with Grandpa. Old though he was, Grandpa was as ready for adventure as Macpherson himself.

"Ship ahoy! Let's be off!" he cried, without

waiting to consider whether it was sensible or not. Aunt Janet was the one to think of that!

"At your time of life!" she cried out. "Have you no sense?"

Grandpa wagged his beard at her and said, "What could be more sensible than going off into the fresh air? It'll put new life into us."

"That's right, Grandpa!" agreed Macpherson.

"Oh, you!" Aunt Janet rounded on him; but what was the use? The pair of them, united together, were too much for her.

"Janet woman, you're beaten!" said the old man. "What about packing up and coming with us?"

"Me!" sniffed Aunt Janet. "I'd as soon fly to the moon on a broomstick."

"Now, there's an idea!" chuckled Grandpa; but Aunt Janet would not listen to any more nonsense. She stumped off, shaking her head and vowing: "You'll live to regret it. But nobody listens to me. What's the use of talking sense to you two?"

No use, at all!

They had no intention, of course, of taking wee Maisie Murphy with them. She just came! She climbed up into the caravan, with the kitten in her arms, and that was that.

"Here! Get down, Maisie," said Macpherson crossly. "You can't come with us."

"I can tho!" said Maisie, settling into her seat.

"Let the lassie come," said Grandpa, making room for her. "Wait now, Maisie! Maybe you'd better go and get some things."

"What kind of thingth?" asked Maisie, looking up at him.

"Clothes," said Grandpa.

"Okay! I'll go and get them. You hold Thnowy." She thrust Snowy into the old man's arms, scrambled down and trotted off into the Murphies' overcrowded house.

A few moments later she came back with an untidy bundle and a brood of young Murphies at her heels.

"You're to be ever tho good while I'm away," she told them severely. "I'll be back in time for the baby."

Yet another one was due; but the more the merrier as far as Maisie was concerned. She would have liked to take the latest ones with her. The twins—Him and Her—were sitting on the doorstep sucking their thumbs for want of anything else. But both Grandpa and Macpherson were firm. If she must have something to nurse, she could take the kitten.

No babies allowed on board the caravan!

The entire brood broke into howls when they saw they were being left behind. Maisie joined in, to keep them company; but her tears soon dried when they set off and she felt the jolting movement of the caravan. Maisie always threw herself heart and soul into any new experience. It was fun to be on the move, away from the dingy Tenements, with her hero sitting beside her.

"Merthy! it'th like being on a theethaw!" she cried, her face beaming with delight. "Gee-up, pony!"

"Sit still!" Macpherson warned her. "And don't speak to the pony. You'll put him off his stride."

"Okay Macpherthon! Whatever you thay!"

They were rattling out into the main stream of traffic. Grandpa held tightly to the reins and did his best to steer Slow-Coach safely through. The pony did not seem to like the noisy buses and motor cars. He tossed his head, snorted down his nose and whisked his tail uneasily.

"Steady, boy, steady!" said Grandpa, soothingly. "Heave ho, my hearty!"

The Highland policeman was holding them up at a crossing. He pushed back his helmet in surprise when he saw who was perched up on the caravan. "Man, Macpherson, is it yourself? There's no knowing what you'll be doing next! Where would you be off to, now?"

"It's a mystery-tour!" said Macpherson, grinning down at him. "Keep an eye on Glasgow till I get back."

"I'll do that!" The policeman patted the pony and waved them on. "Away you go, Macpherson, and the best of luck."

They needed plenty of luck to get through the traffic. The cars and buses and vans and lorries and motor-cycles seemed to be coming at them from all sides. It was not easy to weave a way through. There was not much talking except to the pony. "Steady, Slow-Coach! Ship ahoy! Watch your step!"

Even Maisie was silent until they left the traffic behind. Then she turned to her hero and asked, "Where are we going, Macpherthon?"

"Wait and see! Stop asking silly questions."

"Okay, Macpherthon!"

What did it matter where they were going as long as *he* was there? If it came to that, none of them knew where they were going. They had no map, no plans, no rules.

"We'll just follow the road signs," said Grandpa, trying to steer the pony as if it was a ship. "We'll get off the main road soon, and then it's over to you, Macpherson!"

It was a happy moment for Macpherson when he first took the reins in his hand. He was a Sheikh driving in state! Superman flying through the stratosphere! He was the King of the Gypsies going to his coronation!

Grandpa sat back and lit his pipe while Slow-Coach broke into a canter. Up-and-down! Up-and-down! Sometimes they were jolted sideways for a change, with Maisie hanging on to her hat.

The hat had once been her mother's Sunday best, with a feather on one side and a bunch of roses on the other. It was several sizes too big for Maisie, but she was used to that. Everything she wore was either too big or too small. It was seldom, if ever, that she wore anything new.

"What about some grub?" said Grandpa when they had been jogging along for another mile or two. The pony had slowed down and was showing signs of tiring. "Better give Slow-Coach a rest. Draw in to the side, Macpherson, and we'll see what's on the menu. Are you feeling peckish, Maisie?"

"Yeth, I am!" No need to ask! Maisie was always peckish. "Ith it dinner or tea or thupper?"

"Well now, that's a question! It might be the whole lot rolled into one," said Grandpa, his eyes twinkling. "Hop down, and let's have a look at the larder."

The larder, such as it was, had been as unplanned as the journey. Indeed, it might have been as empty as Mother Hubbard's cupboard had it not been for Mr Grim's food-hamper. He and Miss Peacock had packed it between them. Now it was stowed away in the back of the caravan, along with a bag of corn for Slow-Coach.

"A going-away present, Macpherson, me boy!" Mr Grim winked at him. "It's a hungry job travelling round the world. I remember when I was in the Sahara Desert and me camel went lame...."

They found all sorts of treasures inside the hamper, enough to keep them going for days, if not weeks. Eggs, bacon, sausages, bread, biscuits, tea, sugar, milk. There were some "extras", too: a packet of tobacco, a box of sweets, a bag full of apples and oranges, and a cake with MANY HAPPY RETURNS on top, though it was nobody's birthday.

"Perhapth it'th the pony'th," said Maisie, looking longingly at the pink icing.

"You're daft!" said Macpherson, keeping

Maisie in her place. He was fond of her, but he had no intention of showing it.

As for the pony, whether it was his birthday or not, he seemed to know how to fend for himself. He had begun to crop the grass at the side of the road, raising his head now and again to give a contented whinny.

"He'd sooner have that than the birthday-cake," said Grandpa, patting Slow-Coach's piebald coat. "Hold on, old fellow, and you'll soon have your next course. Wait till I put some corn in your nose-bag."

Soon they were all as busy as bees. Grandpa lit the stove. Macpherson acted as head cook. Maisie spread a cloth and laid out the cups and plates; and before long the bacon and sausages were sizzling merrily in the frying-pan.

"Oh my! It thmellth awful good," said Maisie, wrinkling up her nose.

It tasted even better! It was a wonderful feast—their first meal by the wayside. The fresh air had sharpened their appetites. After eating big helpings of bacon, eggs and sausages, they were still hungry. Macpherson pounced on an apple pie which he found in the food-hamper. They each had a chunk, followed by slices of birthday cake, and ending with cheese for Grandpa, fruit for Macpherson and Maisie, and a saucerful of milk for Snowy.

They finished off their mugs of tea. At long last even Maisie admitted, "I'm full! If I eat any more I'll burtht!"

They were relaxing on the grass, half asleep, when a sudden strange sound came from behind them. The kitten gave a frightened "Miaow" and leapt for safety into Maisie's arms. Slow-Coach pricked up his ears and began to snort with alarm.

"D-Did you hear that, Grandpa?" asked Macpherson, afraid to look round.

"I did, my boy," said Grandpa drowsily. "What would you say it was?"

"It sounded like a—a wild beast."

"Merthy me!" cried Maisie, clutching Snowy closer to her; but, in spite of her fear, she swung round to look. Then she gave a sigh of relief. "It'th okay! Look Macpherthon! It'th only a big cat."

Macpherson turned round. Then he sprang to his feet and said in a shaky voice, "It's not a big cat. It's a tiger!"

"Nonsense!" said Grandpa, calmly smoking his pipe. "Steady on, Macpherson! Can't be tigers in these parts. We're still in Scotland, not India. . . ."

Just then the big cat let out a loud roar.

"Shiver me timbers!" gasped Grandpa and struggled to his feet. It was a tiger all right! He had seen plenty of them before, but never quite as close as this.

It was a relief to see that there was a chain round the animal's neck, and that a man had it firmly in control. All the same, it was a startling sight to see in a quiet roadway. No wonder Snowy's fur was standing on end and that Maisie shrank back, calling out: "Keep him away! Don't let him eat uth! Oh my! I've never theen a cat ath big ath that!"

The man threw back his head and laughed. He was small and dark-skinned, with a deep scar on his face. When he spoke it was in a broad Scots accent mixed up with a foreign tongue.

"He no big cat! He big tiger! Tarzan the Tiger—from the menagerie."

Maisie stared—first at the big cat and then at the little man. "What'th a menagerie?" she asked.

"It's beasts," said the little man, tugging the tiger back. Tarzan had caught sight of the birthday cake and seemed eager to sample it. "We gotta lotta beasts in the menagerie. We gotta seals. We gotta snakes...."

"Where?" Maisie wanted to know.

"Round-a corner," said the little man, looking over his shoulder. "We broke-a down. Mistress Mackay, she mend-a the lorry. Mistress Mackay, she can mend-a anything."

He said it in a half proud and half fearful manner. He was not afraid of wild beasts, but it seemed that Mistress Mackay could make him tremble!

"Does she own the menagerie?" It was Grandpa's turn to ask a question.

"Ay, sure she does. Mistress Mackay's Menagerie." The little man took another cautious look over his shoulder. "She own me, too! I am the husband-man. But she no like-a my name. Pietro Poppelini. No good! She call-a me ...."

"Pietro Mackay!"

Even the tiger cringed at the sound of her voice. It was no ordinary voice. It was deeper than a man's; louder than any fog-horn. As for Pietro, he seemed to go to pieces. His hands began to shake. His face started to twitch, and his voice was trembling when he called back: "Yes-yes-yes-yes! Here am I, Mistress Mackay! Round-a corner!"

"Come on! The lorry's mended! What are you up to?"

Before he could reply she appeared round

the corner like a whirlwind. Pietro and the tiger kept close together, as if for protection. But there was no escaping from Mistress Mackay!

4

Adventures All the Way

"*Tarzan! Pietro! Come on!*"

She was the biggest woman Macpherson had ever seen—a great mountain of a woman—dressed in dungarees, with a man's beret stuck on top of her untidy hair. Her face was weather-beaten, her arms powerful; her feet, in big boots, seemed almost twice the size of her husband's. Indeed, Pietro appeared to grow smaller the nearer she came to him.

"What's been going on?" She caught him by the scruff of the neck as if he were a puppet on a string. "I can't let you out of my sight!"

"Mistress Mackay! Mistress Mackay! I no do anythings wrong! I take-a the tiger for the walk. I meet-a these nice-a peoples. . . ."

"Hullo!" said Grandpa, thinking it was time he entered into the conversation. "How d'you do?"

"*How do I do?*" She swung round and glared fiercely at Grandpa. "I would do a lot better if this good-for-nothing man would get a move on. He's more bother than the tiger."

"Grrrrrrrr!"

At that moment Tarzan lunged forward and tried to take a bite out of the birthday cake.

"Watch-a out!" warned Pietro in a squeaky voice. He was still in his wife's clutches and did not find it easy to speak. "He gobble-a it all up."

Macpherson rescued the cake while Grandpa made a suggestion. "Why not have some cake yourself, Pietro; and you, too, Mrs Mackay? There's still plenty of tea left in the pot."

The big woman suddenly let go of her husband and squatted down on the grass. "I might as well. Pour me out a cup."

"That's her!" said Pietro, sighing with relief. "Up in the air or down in the dust-a! Very strange woman, Mistress Mackay!"

His wife took no notice of him, but accepted a large chunk of cake and a mugful of tea. Then she began to talk to Grandpa in her powerful voice. *"What's your line? Are you in the business?"*

"No, no," said Grandpa. "We're just on holiday."

"Lucky you! No holiday for me, with a lazy lout like Pietro!" She gave her husband a

playful push which sent him sprawling back
over in the grass. Then suddenly she wiped her
mouth with the back of her hand and rose to
her feet. "Come on, round the corner, the lot of
you. Come and see the menagerie."

Macpherson, for one, needed no second
invitation. He was round the corner in a
twinkling—and there it was, a ramshackle
lorry with a trailer hitched on to the back. On
the side was painted in large letters: MISTRESS
MACKAY'S MENAGERIE.

"Where are the animals?" asked Macpherson, peering over the side.

He drew back quickly when a seal popped its head up from a tank. At the same time, a monkey leapt up into the driving seat and put its paws on the wheel as if ready to drive off. Macpherson could see snakes writhing about in another tank in the trailer, and a cage full of white mice, twirling merrily round and round on a little treadmill.

"Let *me* thee!" cried Maisie, jumping up and down with excitement. "Oh my! Ithn't it great!" She could have gazed for ever at the white mice; but something else caught her eye. "What'th that?"

It was a bundle in a corner of the lorry—a bundle that was beginning to stir.

"The bambino!" said Pietro, lifting up the bundle and showing it to Maisie. "Look-a! He give-a the smile to his papa! I call-a him Gino. Mistress Mackay she no like-a the name. She call him Willy."

It did not matter to Maisie what he was called. He was a baby and that was enough for her. "Come on, you," she said, stretching out her arms. "Diddle-diddle-dumpling!"

Maisie sat down on the roadside dangling the plump bambino in her arms, while Mrs

Mackay bundled the tiger back into the trailer. All the time she kept shouting at her husband.

"*Pietro Mackay!* Get a move on! Help me with this rope! *Do you hear me?* What a useless creature you are! The monkey's got more sense!"

Grandpa and Macpherson lent a hand while Pietro told them: "She no mean-a half the things she say. Very strange woman, Mistress Mackay!"

Indeed, they were both strange, yet somehow they seemed to fit into the odd life they led, roaming the countryside like wandering tinkers.

"Maybe we'll meet again," said Grandpa, when the creaking lorry was ready to set off.

"Maybe yes and maybe no," shouted Mrs Mackay, pushing the monkey out of the driving seat. "*Pietro Mackay! Come on!* What's up now?"

"The bambino! He no want-a to come!"

Gino—or Willy—had set up a howl on being parted from Maisie. Her lip was beginning to tremble, too. The tiger growled in sympathy; the monkey chattered; the lorry backfired; and the air was filled with din as they finally set off in a cloud of dust.

"Ta-ta, you!" Maisie waved to the tearful

baby. "Do you think we'll ever thee them again?" she asked.

"Yes, we will, my dear," said Grandpa, gripping her small hand. "I've got a feeling in my bones that we'll meet again soon. Come along, my hearties! Time for us to move on. Yoke the pony, Macpherson!"

"Ay, ay, sir!" Macpherson gave a smart salute and went scurrying round the corner. He came back again in a few seconds, looking startled.

"What's up, my boy?"

"He's not there! Slow-Coach! He's gone!"

"Merthy me!" Maisie tugged Grandpa round the corner, eager to find out if it was true. The deserted caravan was there—but no sign of the pony.

"I should have had the sense to tether him," Grandpa reproached himself. "Surely he can't have gone far. Have you looked in the field, Macpherson?"

"No, I haven't. The gate's not open. Slow-Coach could never have jumped over."

"Oh yeth, he could!" Maisie, half over the fence herself, pointed to the middle of the field—and there was the pony calmly cropping the grass. Some cows were feeding beside him, taking no notice of a stranger in their midst.

"That beats all!" cried Grandpa. "Off you go, Macpherson, and bring him back. Maisie can stay with me and help to pack up."

They had finished their task long before Macpherson had made any progress. Slow-Coach was in no mood to leave the field. This was the life for him! No work to do! Plenty to eat! What more could he want?

"Come on, Slow-Coach, that's a good fellow. Back to the caravan!"

The pony took no notice, apart from moving out of Macpherson's reach to crop a fresh patch of grass. No amount of pushing or prodding would make him change his mind. As far as Slow-Coach was concerned, he was in the field for life.

Macpherson had almost given up hope when a dog came bounding over the fence, followed more slowly by a man with a gun under his arm. He gave an angry shout when he saw the boy. "Hi, you! What are you doing in my field?"

He glared first at Macpherson and then at the pony. "What's this beast doing here? Get out, the pair of you, or I'll shoot you both."

It was only a threat. Macpherson was sure that the man had no intention of firing the gun. All the same, it was best not to take risks.

"S-Sorry, s-sir! You s-see ..."

"I don't see anything except trespassers in my field. Get out before I lose my temper."

It seemed, by the angry flush on his face, that his temper was lost already. As for getting out of the field, Macpherson was only too willing; but how could he go without Slow-Coach? The pony had wandered off and found a soft patch of grass where he lay down and settled himself for a sleep; but it was to be a short sleep! The man snapped his fingers angrily and rapped out an order to the dog who came yelping across the field towards his target.

Slow-Coach was up in a twinkling. With the dog snapping at his heels, he set off at a gallop towards the fence. Macpherson watched in amazement. He had no idea that the pony could move so quickly. With a sudden leap Slow-Coach was over the fence, landing safely beside the caravan.

Macpherson wasted no time in hurrying after him, while the man called out angrily: "If I ever see you here again, young fellow, I'll shoot...."

Bang!

The gun went off with a loud explosion. Macpherson's heart almost stopped beating.

He stood stock-still, not knowing whether he
had been shot or not. He felt no pain; he could
see no blood. Yet his ears were ringing....

"Those thieving crows! I'll shoot the lot of
them...."

Macpherson breathed again. He turned
hastily round to see the man aiming his gun
into the air. Thank goodness, *he* was not a
crow!

"Oh Macpherthon! Are you all right?"

called Maisie, who was hanging over the fence waiting for him to come back. "I thought that bad man wath going to kill you."

"Don't be silly!" said Macpherson crossly—but his heart was still thumping.

"Heave ho!" cried Grandpa, yoking Slow-Coach to the caravan. "At least, we've learnt one lesson, Macpherson, my boy. We'll never let *him* loose again!"

"Where are we going to thleep tonight?"

Maisie was half-asleep already, jolting up and down as she sat between Grandpa and Macpherson with the kitten still clutched in her arms. It had been a long, exciting day for her. She had almost forgotten what Glasgow, and even the twins looked like. It seemed as if she had been jogging along behind the piebald pony all her life.

Where would they sleep? It was a question that had crossed Grandpa's mind, too. It was beginning to grow dark and they were all ready for bed. The pony had slowed down and was stumbling along at a snail's pace. Even Macpherson, who was holding the reins, was having difficulty in keeping awake.

"Can't we just stop and pitch the tent anywhere?" he yawned.

"No, no, my boy. We can't be like Slow-

Coach and stray on to other people's property," Grandpa warned him. "We'll have to get permission."

The trouble was, they could find no one to ask. They were on a long lonely stretch of road with not a house in sight. There was not even a passer-by to be seen. Certainly there were plenty of fields where they could have camped in comfort, but Grandpa was not risking an encounter with another angry farmer.

"Keep your eyes open, Macpherson," said the old man, taking over the reins. "At the first sign of life, we'll stop and try our luck. Ahoy there, Slow-Coach! Put on a spurt!"

Grandpa began to sing a sea-shanty to liven them all up. For a while the pony's pace grew brisker, but not for long. Suddenly, he whisked his tail, gave a snort of protest and came to a full-stop.

"Oh dear! That's him gone on strike," said Macpherson, jumping down. "Wake up, old boy! You'll soon be having a rest."

Slow-Coach shook himself awake and stepped out once more with Macpherson leading him. It was slow progress. The pony was now so unsteady on his feet that there was no knowing when he might try to lie down. The sun was sinking low in the sky, and still there was no sign of life.

Then suddenly Maisie gave them the good news. "Oh look!" she cried sleepily. "I thee a thtar!"

"A star?" Grandpa had studied the stars often enough when he was sailing the seas. "That's not a star, my dear. It's a light."

"Hooray!" cried Macpherson, perking up. "We'll make straight for it. Come on, Slow-Coach!"

The light came from a small cottage by the roadside, with big gates nearby leading up to a drive.

"It's a lodge-house," said Grandpa, as they drew nearer. "There must be a big house, or maybe a castle, in the grounds. Knock at the door, Macpherson, and ask if we can camp in one of the fields."

It was a long time before anyone answered his knock. When the door finally opened, Macpherson saw the cause for the delay. An old woman in a wheelchair sat there peering out at him and asking in a shaky voice: "Who's there? What's up? Is there anything wrong?"

"No, there's nothing wrong," said Macpherson soothingly. "We just want permission to camp for the night. You see, we're in a caravan. There's Grandpa and wee Maisie

Murphy and the pony and we're awful tired . . ."

The whole story came out while he stood on the doorstep and the old lady stared over his head at Grandpa and Maisie in the caravan. She seemed to like the look of them, for she interrupted Macpherson and called out: "Open the gate and drive through. You can camp in the grounds. The Lord's away."

"The Lord?" Macpherson stared at her.

"Lord Wallace. He lives up there in the big house. But he's abroad just now, and there's only Jimmy there—my nephew. He's the caretaker. My name's Mrs Smith. Pleased to meet you all. I tell you what, when you've unyoked the pony, come inside and have your supper. I could do with a bit of company. I don't get about much."

She went creaking away in her wheelchair while Macpherson gave Grandpa the thumbs-up signal. They had struck lucky!

"Merthy me! What a lot of dogth you've got!"

There were half a dozen of them on the mantelpiece, all made of china. They stared solemnly down at Maisie as she sat on a small stool with Snowy curled up beside her on the rug. Mrs Smith was wheeling herself round the kitchen, laying the table and taking a look now and then at the pots by the fire.

"Cocky-leekie soup," she said. "It's lucky I made a big potful. Jimmy comes down for his dinner every day, but there's plenty left over. I've put a pie in the oven, and the kettle's boiling."

"It'th awful kind of you," said Maisie, still staring at the china dogs.

"Oh, I like company. I tell you what, lassie; there's a spare bed upstairs. Would you like to sleep there tonight?"

"Yeth, I would!"

"That's fine! I'll give you a pig to put in the bed."

"Oh no, thankth!" Maisie sat up on her stool, looking alarmed. "I don't think I like pigth in the bed."

Mrs Smith laughed. "It's only a stone hot-water-bottle. Keeps in the heat all night. That's the old name for it—a pig."

"Fanthy!" Maisie was learning a lot on her travels. By the time Grandpa and Macpherson came knocking at the door she and Mrs Smith were firm friends. She had explored the little cottage, both upstairs and down. She had helped her hostess to get the meal ready. She had counted the china dogs and admired the wax fruit under its glass cover. She knew everything that was in the cupboards, and where to find the knives and forks and the cups and saucers.

"Come in, Grandpa and Macpherthon," she cried, as if *she* were the hostess. "The thupper'th ready, and I'm going to thleep here tonight. With a pig!"

5

The Midnight Burglar

They were all fast asleep. Maisie was snuggled up to her cosy pig in the little cottage bedroom. Grandpa and Macpherson were every bit as snug in their tent in the grounds. Slow-Coach had found a soft resting-place near by. Not a sound was heard except the rustle of the trees and the hooting of an owl in the woods.

Mrs Smith had entertained them, not only with food, but with stories of the big house in which the Lord lived. As they supped their soup, she told them of the treasures he had collected. The house was full of rare pictures, valuable silver and old relics belonging to his ancestors.

"Are you not afraid of burglars, with him away?" asked Grandpa, emptying his plate.

Mrs Smith wheeled herself to the pot by the fire to give him a second helping. "Not with Jimmy there! He's an all-in wrestler is Jimmy. Battling Jimmy Smith, they call him! The Lord never worries about his treasures as long as Jimmy's in charge."

She went on to tell them tales about her nephew's adventures in the wrestling-ring, while she served them with steak-and-kidney pie. By the end of the meal, when their stomachs were full and their eyes nearly closing, Macpherson—half-asleep—was ready to dream about body-blows and burglars.

As he lay beside Grandpa in the tent, he drifted quickly off to sleep. But he woke with a start when he heard a noise like a loud explosion.

"What's that, Grandpa?" he cried, sitting bolt upright and rubbing his eyes; but the old man was too sound asleep to hear anything.

Macpherson sat and listened, with his heart thumping. No sound! "I must have been dreaming," he thought, and was about to settle down again when another explosion, louder than the first, was heard overhead. A crack of thunder!

Macpherson gave a sigh of relief. Now that he knew what it was, he was content to go back to sleep. But not when he heard the other sound!

It was a sinister, shuffling sound outside the tent. Someone was moving stealthily in the grounds. Macpherson could hear footsteps. He could hear twigs crackling on the ground. He

could hear heavy breathing. Was it his own, or did it come from someone outside?

A burglar! This was the first thought in Macpherson's mind. Without disturbing Grandpa, he wriggled out of his sleeping-bag, put on his coat and went out into the night.

At first he could see nothing except the shadowy figure of Slow-Coach asleep beside the caravan. All was dark and quiet at the cottage. The thunder was still rumbling in the distance, growing fainter as the storm passed over. Then, suddenly, he saw the stealthy figure moving along a pathway leading to the big house.

What was he to do? Run up to the house by a roundabout way and warn Mrs Smith's nephew that a prowler was lurking in the grounds? He would have to be quick and quiet. The man must not suspect that anyone had seen him.

Macpherson, Super-Spy, braced himself and set off through the dark wood, trying to keep the man in sight without being seen or heard himself. He must make a detour and then run like a hare to raise the alarm.

It was a pity that the Super-Spy did not notice the old tree-trunk in front of him. Macpherson stumbled over it and fell to the ground with a crash. He was up again in a twinkling, but the damage had been done. The man whipped round, let out a shout and came rushing at him with his fists clenched.

Macpherson's first instinct was to turn and run. Safety first! But what would Grandpa think of him if he acted in such a cowardly fashion? And what would happen to Lord Wallace's treasures if he did not stop the man?

The Super-Spy acted on his second impulse. He had no time to think out a plan. He just rushed forward to meet the man, then did a swift tackle and caught him round the knees. Both of them came crashing to the ground with

Macpherson on top.

"Grandpa! Help!" he called, trying to hold the man down; but already the intruder had wriggled round and caught him by the throat.

"What do you think you're up to?" he roared, holding the boy in a grip of iron. He peered at Macpherson through the darkness. Then, suddenly, he relaxed his grip and cried: "Bless my soul! This is the first time I've been brought down by anyone your size! Congratulations, my lad! You've got the makings of a fine all-in wrestler!"

"Mercy me!" gasped Macpherson, struggling to his feet. "You're not Battling Jimmy Smith?"

"The very same!" The man stood up, flexing his muscles. Even in the dim light Macpherson could see how burly he was. Imagine tackling *him!*

"I'm s-sorry, Mr S-Smith! I thought you were a burglar!"

"That's all right, chum! I'm used to rough handling; but not from someone your size! You'll be Macpherson? My aunt rang me from the cottage to say you were camping here. I thought I'd take a look round before settling for the night. Can't be too careful with strangers about—but I needn't have worried!"

"Oh dear!" Macpherson was still dismayed at what he had done. "You see, your aunt was telling us all about the treasures in the big house, and when I heard someone moving about . . ."

"No need to worry, chum! Better be safe than sorry. Talking about treasures, how would you like to come and see them?"

"Now?"

"Sure! Why not? You can see some of my trophies as well. The ones I won at wrestling."

"Okay!" said Macpherson, delighted at the prospect. He was too wide awake by now to think of going back to sleep. It was not every day—or every night—that he had the chance to meet a champion wrestler.

They set off together along a narrow pathway leading to the big house. The thunder was still rolling and rumbling away in the distance. Then suddenly the sky lightened. The moon shone out and Macpherson caught a glimpse of a rambling old castle with turrets and towers. He saw something else, too; something moving in front of them! An animal? Or a human being?

"See," he whispered to his companion. "What's that?"

Battling Jimmy Smith stiffened. "Someone

prowling in the grounds! *He's* up to no good!"

Macpherson's heart began to thump with excitement. There was no mistake this time! They were on the trail of a real burglar.

"Could you do it again, chum?"

"What? Tackle him?"

"That's it! Nip up behind and take him by surprise. I'll be ready to do the rest."

"I'll t-try!"

It was the most exciting moment of Macpherson's life. Wait till Grandpa heard about it! He moved off swiftly and silently. This time he must not miss his footing. He crept nearer and nearer to the man while Battling Jimmy Smith hurried off in the opposite direction, trying to bar the burglar's way to the big house.

Suddenly, the man stopped, as if he sensed danger in the air. His hand went quickly to his pocket and whipped something out. Macpherson turned pale when he saw it shining in the moonlight. A gun!

It was at this point that Jimmy Smith loomed up in front of the burglar, hoping to take him by surprise. But it was he who got the surprise when he saw a gun being levelled at him.

"Look out!"

Macpherson gave a yell and acted quickly. He lunged forward, dived at the man's legs and brought him down with a crash.

"Come on, Thleepy-Head! Wake up!"

Macpherson was in a sound sleep next morning when Maisie came into the tent and tried to shake him awake. Grandpa was already up and about, feeding Slow-Coach and getting ready for the day's journey.

No one else had heard a sound during the night. Macpherson's tale seemed like part of a dream, or a nightmare. As he sat at breakfast in Mrs Smith's cosy kitchen, he told them all about it.

"I had to dial 999! Then the police came and took the burglar away," he said proudly. "After that Mr Jimmy took me round the house and showed me all the trophies he had won and all the Lord's treasures; and then he made me some tea."

"Merthy me!" Maisie looked at him admiringly. There was no end to Macpherson's adventures, even in the middle of the night. "Did you get anything to eat?" Food interested Maisie more than burglars!

Macpherson, to tease her, turned the midnight snack into a feast. "We had turkey and chicken and trifle and chocolate cake and ice-cream...."

"Ithe-cream!" Maisie's eyes grew rounder. "You might have wakened me up, Macpherthon!"

"Now then," said Grandpa, shaking his head at the boy. "Tell the truth, Macpherson."

"We just had a plain biscuit," confessed the boy, coming down to earth. "I was too excited to eat. You should have seen the size of the burglar...."

He was off again! Mrs Smith tried to turn his attention towards his boiled egg and toast. "Eat, boy, eat! You've got a long journey in front of you."

Battling Jimmy Smith himself called in at the cottage to confirm Macpherson's story. He brought with him a large basket full of fruit from the Lord's garden, and some new-laid eggs.

"I shouldn't be surprised if there's a reward coming your way for what you did last night," he told Macpherson. "Sergeant Brown was saying they'd been after that man for months."

"Goodness gracious!" Macpherson felt that he had already had enough reward. "You mean money?"

"Likely enough. You'd better leave your

address, chum."

"I haven't got one. I don't know where we're going."

"He means your home address, Macpherson," said Grandpa. "It's Number Five, Clyde-View Tenements, Glasgow." The old man heaved himself up out of his chair and turned to Mrs Smith. "We'd better be on our way. Thank you, ma'am, for all your kindness. We'll never forget it."

"Wait!" She wheeled herself round the kitchen, opening drawers and cupboards and bringing out paper bags which she filled with scones and biscuits and gingerbread. Then she found a small pot of strawberry jam to give to Maisie. Finally, she waved them off at the door, calling: "Come again! I've enjoyed your visit!"

They were off!

Macpherson soon forgot his sleepiness when he felt the tang of the fresh morning air. Slow-Coach stepped out briskly, and before long they reached the outskirts of a small village.

"Let's stop and send postcards," suggested Macpherson.

They needed one for Aunt Janet; another for Miss Peacock; a funny one for Mr Grim, and a thank-you card for old Mrs Smith.

"Maybe we'd better buy one for Old Skinflint, too," said Macpherson, trying to find something suitable. In the end he chose a plain postcard and wrote: *Having a nice time.* He was about to add: "Wish you were here", but stopped himself in time from telling such a downright lie. Instead, he changed it to: *Hope you are feeling better. See you soon!*

But not too soon! There was still the open road before them, and days and days of freedom.

"Which way, my hearties?" asked Grandpa when they reached the crossroads outside the village. "North, south, east or west?"

Macpherson studied the signpost. "Let's go south," he suggested. "Maybe we could cross into England. I've never been there before."

"Ith it a foreign country?" asked Maisie, with visions of savages and wild beasts roaming in the jungle.

"No; not as foreign as all that," said Grandpa, smiling at her. "Let's go and find out."

"Right!" said Macpherson, picking up the reins. "Gee-up, Slow-Coach! Forward march!"

It was exciting following the signposts and finding themselves coming nearer and nearer to a new country. At every turn of the road there

was something interesting to see. When they reached the next village they found a great stir going on.

"Ship ahoy! Pull up, Macpherson!" called Grandpa. "I've heard *that* voice before."

They could all hear it now, loud and clear.

"*Pietro Mackay! What are you doing?*"

"I feed-a the tiger, Mistress Mackay. I brush-a his coat. Make-a him look-a beautiful ..."

"I'll make you look beautiful if you don't hurry up. *Get a move on!*"

The voice echoed up and down the village street. There was no mistaking it. Mistress Mackay was on the rampage!

She and her husband had set up the menagerie on the village green. Shoals of children were crowding round, eager to see the seals performing and to watch the antics of the monkey.

"Let's stop and watch, too. May we, Grandpa?" asked Macpherson, tugging at the reins.

"Why not?" Grandpa was always ready for a new adventure. "There's nothing to hurry us. Have you got any money, Macpherson? You'll have to pay."

"Oh yes, Grandpa. I've got thousands." Not quite thousands, if the truth was told. Macpherson had ninepence which he had saved up for the journey, and a shining fifty pence piece which Mr Grim had given him on parting. Grandpa was the one who held the real purse-strings. He had sold some of his ships-in-bottles before he left, and had several pound notes hidden away in a safe place.

"No! Not-a one penny from you! You have the free-look-a," cried Pietro, when he saw them approach the menagerie, ready to pay. "Welcome, my good-a friends! Is nice to see you again."

He looked over his shoulder and lowered his voice. "Mistress Mackay, she make-a the big noise. Always she give-a me the scoldings . . ."

"*Pietro Mackay! Let's get started!*"

Macpherson and the others stood on the outskirts of the crowd to watch the performance. They had already had a private view, and almost felt as if they belonged to the menagerie—but they had a special treat when they saw Mrs Mackay in action.

The crowd gasped as she lifted up the snakes and curled them round her powerful arms and neck. Pietro stood by, clapping his hands and calling: "Bravo! Well-a done, Mistress Mackay! She is the brave-a woman!"

Then it was his turn—and the seals'—to perform. He bounced big red balls at them which the creatures balanced on their snouts. They flapped their flippers and tossed the balls to each other as if playing a game, while the children, looking on, laughed and cheered.

There was no need for Tarzan the Tiger to perform. He just stood still and looked fierce! Now and again he gave a roar which made the children shrink back in alarm. But they liked him! Some even ventured near enough to pat him.

"He no do you no harm-a," Pietro assured them. "When he give the roar, he only saying big Hullo-a!"

The monkey was the greatest favourite of all. Grandpa and Macpherson, along with the rest, were so absorbed in watching his comical capers that they did not notice Maisie's disappearance.

"Where on earth has she gone?" said Macpherson, at the end of the performance.

The monkey had taken its final leap into Pietro's arms and Mrs Mackay was already packing everything back into the lorry.

"Silly thing!" said Macpherson. "Lassies are the limit!"

"Maybe she's gone back to the caravan," suggested Grandpa, making his way towards it as fast as his stiff old legs would take him. He had been careful this time to tie the pony to a post. Slow-Coach was peacefully cropping the grass on the green, but there was no sign of Maisie.

"Wait, Grandpa! I've got an idea!" cried Macpherson. "You know her! She'll likely have gone to look at that baby."

Macpherson pushed his way through the crowds towards the Mackays' lorry. The bambino was there all right, lying sucking his thumb and looking plumper than ever. But no Maisie!

6

The Fun of the Fair

Grandpa and Macpherson were at the end of
their tether. They had searched high and low;
up and down the village street, in and out of
every shop; now they had come back to the
caravan in despair.

"What'll we do, Grandpa?" asked Macpherson hopelessly. He was worried now, instead of
angry with Maisie. If only she would come
back he would never say another cross word to
her. "Poor wee soul! What can have happened? Oh, Grandpa, you don't think she's
been kidnapped?"

"No, no," said Grandpa, soothingly. Suddenly he made a discovery. "Ship ahoy!
Where's Snowy? *She's* missing, too!"

"Oh, goodness, so she is! She must have
wandered off, and Maisie's gone to look for
her." Macpherson felt a little less worried
now that he could see a cause for Maisie's
disappearance.

"They can't have gone far. Let's have

another look," suggested Grandpa. "You run on ahead, Macpherson. I'll bring up the rear. My old pins are a bit shaky."

Macpherson sped away down the village street. Beyond the shops and the houses, he could see a river rushing along on its way to the sea. He stopped suddenly in his tracks when he caught sight of a little group by the river bank, all shouting and talking excitedly. Two big boys were there; they seemed to be hauling something out of the water.

Macpherson's face went white. What if it was Maisie? As he rushed forward he saw something lying on the ground—a hat with its feathers and flowers all bedraggled. Maisie's hat!

"*Maisie!*"

He gave a frantic shout and ran towards the river bank. Putting on a spurt, he arrived there just in time to help to haul her out.

"Oh Macpherthon!" She clung to his hand, dripping wet and soaked to the skin; but it was not her own plight that troubled her. "Thnowy! Where'th Thnowy? Oh Macpherthon! They've gone and drownded her!"

"No, we haven't," said one of the big boys, looking sheepish. "It was just for fun."

"Fun!" Macpherson whipped round on him

with the light of battle in his eyes. He looked so fierce that the boy, big though he was, shrank back out of reach.

"We didn't think she would believe us," he mumbled. "We put the kitten in a sack and pretended to throw it into the river, but it was another sack, full of stones. It was just to tease her! We never thought the lassie would go in after it."

The lassie faced up to him in a fury. "Where'th Thnowy? What have you done to her? If you've hurted her I'll—I'll *kill* you. Tho I will!"

She put up her small fists as if ready to fight to the death. She looked a sight with her draggled hair and dripping clothes, but Macpherson had never felt so fond of her. He was so furious at her tormentors that he, too, could have killed them.

"Come on! Tell her where the kitten is! Any more nonsense and I'll fetch the police," he threatened.

The boys retreated out of his reach; and it was then that he noticed a small sack lying on the bank, with something wriggling inside it. Maisie had noticed it, too, and was on it in a flash.

"Oh Thnowy, you're thafe!" she cried as she

untied the string and brought out the frightened animal, cradling it in her arms and
crooning: "It'th all right! Maithie'll look after
you!"

Maisie's face was beaming with smiles. Now
that the danger was over, her anger against the
boys vanished. Maisie could never keep up a
grudge for long. Unlike Macpherson! *He*
wanted to hit out at someone for having made
her suffer.

"You're not getting away with this! Come on! I'll fight the pair of you!" he challenged them. "I'll throw *you* into the river and see how you like it! I'll give you a good hiding . . ."

"Wait, Macpherson!"

It was Grandpa, laying a restraining hand on the boy's shoulder. He had just arrived on the scene, and it had taken him only a few moments to understand the situation. Grandpa had subtler methods of dealing with it than Macpherson.

"First things first," he said, hauling Maisie to her feet. "This mermaid here'll get her death of cold in these wet clothes. We must get her dried out. What would you suggest?"

He was not asking Macpherson. He was speaking to the big boys, man-to-man, appealing to them for advice. They shuffled their feet and looked shamefaced. Then one of them blurted out: "She could come to our house. It's just up the road."

"Right!" said Grandpa, briskly. "You lead the way. Come on, Miss Mermaid! Forward march!"

Macpherson followed on behind them with a sulky look on his face. Revenge was what *he* wanted. What was Grandpa thinking of, chatting away to Maisie's tormentors as if they

were old friends? After what they had done!
Maisie might have drowned, and Grandpa was
letting them off without a harsh word.

Mrs Swan, the mother of the biggest boy,
was at the door. "Mercy on us!" she cried out.
"The poor lassie's soaking wet! Come in and
I'll get her some dry clothes. How did it
happen?"

This was Macpherson's chance! He was
about to speak up when Grandpa got in before
him.

"Och, you know what young things are like
once they get near the water. They're always
tumbling in. It's very good of you, ma'am to
take the trouble."

"No trouble," said Mrs Swan, hustling
Maisie towards the fireside, where the kitten
settled down on the rug as if she were at home.
"I once had a wee girl myself." Her eyes
strayed sadly to a photograph on the mantelpiece. "I've kept some of her clothes."

Maisie stood on tiptoe to take a closer look
at the little girl with the ringlets and the shy
smile. "What wath her name?" she asked,
putting her wet hand in Mrs Swan's. She
seemed to sense that the girl was no longer
there, except in the picture.

"We called her Jenny," said Mrs Swan as

she smiled at Maisie and squeezed the small hand. "Come along, my dear. I think her clothes will fit you. Better to make use of them than leave them lying about."

While Maisie trotted upstairs with her hostess, Grandpa warmed himself at the fire and talked to the boys who were hanging about uneasily at the open door. Macpherson stood apart, looking sulkier than ever. His fists were clenched, ready for fighting; but the subject, as far as Grandpa was concerned, seemed closed.

The old man was telling the boys about their caravan adventures. "Why not come and see us off? You'll like Slow-Coach! He's full of personality! Wait till you hear what happened when he jumped over the fence...."

Macpherson's looks grew blacker as he saw how the boys were responding to Grandpa's friendly talk. They had gone into the house to be closer to the old man, so that they would not miss anything he said. By now they were so much at ease with him that they were asking eager questions and urging him to continue.

"What happened next? Go on! Tell us some more!"

They were laughing and talking like old friends when Grandpa suddenly broke off. "Ho-ro, up she rises!" he called out. "Macpherson! Come and see this!"

If it had been anyone but Grandpa, Macpherson would have ignored the command. "What's up?" he said in a huffy voice and took his time to make his way into the house. He glared at the boys as he passed them; then stared at a vision who was stepping daintily downstairs.

"Allow me to present a young lady," said Grandpa gallantly. "Miss Maisie Murphy, the caravan Queen!"

For once Maisie was dressed in garments that fitted her. She wore a blue velvet dress with little silver buttons down the front. There was a blue ribbon to match in her hair, and a pair of neat patent-leather shoes on her feet.

"Jings!" gasped Macpherson, forgetting his sulks for the moment. "You look a treat, Maisie!"

"Yeth, tho I do," said Maisie, turning round to let them see the back view. "I'm a real thwell!" There was no false modesty about Maisie!

"You'll be far too grand for the caravan," said Grandpa solemnly.

"Will I?" asked Maisie, looking troubled.

"Nonsense! He's just teasing you," said Mrs Swan, handing a parcel to Grandpa. "There!

I've packed up a skirt and jersey for her. I wanted her to wear them now, but her heart was set on the velvet dress. I must say it suits her."

Maisie's eyes were sparkling. She had forgotten all about her ducking. It was wonderful to be the centre of attraction. Even the big boys were gaping at her in admiration.

"Thankth," she said, looking up at Mrs Swan. "Thankth to Jenny, too," she added, with a glance at the photograph on the mantelpiece.

"That's all right," said Mrs Swan in a husky voice. "I'm sure she'd be pleased."

"Now then, Miss Murphy," said Grandpa, making his way to the door. "Time we were off. Don't forget Snowy."

"Thertainly not!" Maisie picked up the kitten. "Thankth again, Mithith Thwan. I'm ever tho grateful."

Maisie walked carefully up the street in her patent-leather shoes, certain that everyone was looking at her. She was blissfully happy. There was nothing else in the world that she wanted—till she reached the sweet shop and saw the lollipops in the window.

"Oh my! There'th a rathpberry one," she said, pressing her nose to the window pane.

"Come on, you," said Macpherson, impatiently. Even though she was dressed to kill, she was still the same old Maisie, always hankering for sweets. "We've no money to waste on rubbish like that."

Maisie gave him a reproachful look. Imagine calling a raspberry lollipop rubbish! The tears were beginning to well up in her eyes when the two boys, following behind, darted into the shop. They came out a few moments later and thrust a paper bag into Maisie's hands.

"For me?" She peered into the bag. "Merthy! I've got an orange one and a lemon one and a *rathpberry!* Oh thankth!"

Macpherson did not know what to make of it, but Grandpa understood. He nodded at the boys and said, "Come along, lads, and have a look at Slow-Coach. He'll be thinking we've deserted him."

The piebald pony was pawing the ground as if impatient to move off. He let the boys stroke his mane. He even accepted a lick of Maisie's lollipop. All the same he seemed relieved when Macpherson jumped into the driving-seat and gathered up the reins.

Maisie settled down in her seat with the kitten in her arms, looking very elegant in her velvet dress. As Grandpa heaved himself on board, the two boys looked up at him as if they wanted to say something.

"Well, cheerio, my lads," said Grandpa cheerfully.

"Ch-Cheerio!" The biggest boy gave a gulp. "Mister, we're s-sorry!"

"That's all right," said Grandpa, as the caravan moved off. "Watch yourselves!"

That was all! He had never said an angry word to them. "Why not, Grandpa?" asked Macpherson, still sulking a little. "They deserved a good hiding."

"Och, if we all got what we deserved it would be a queer world! Don't worry, my boy! There are more ways than one of teaching a lesson!"

Macpherson looked at the old man with a new respect. Grandpa was right as usual. He always knew! Fighting the boys, or preaching at them, would only have made them angry and resentful. Grandpa's methods were the best. He had got on their side, and been so kind that he had made them feel ashamed. They would remember him and think twice before tormenting anyone again.

"You're great, Grandpa!" said Macpherson, giving him a fond look.

"Oh yes, so I am!" grinned Grandpa. "Ship

ahoy, Macpherson! Here comes the menagerie."

The lorry went skimming past with Pietro waving wildly and Mrs Mackay hooting the horn.

"I hope they thaw me looking my betht," said Maisie, smoothing out her dress.

They were to see her again sooner than Maisie expected. They had jogged only a few miles along the road when they came to a little town. As they reached the outskirts they could tell at once that this was a special day. Flags were flying, bands were playing and everyone was dressed in their best clothes. A banner across the street read: WELCOME TO OUR ANNUAL FAIR.

On the green they saw a familiar sight: Mistress Mackay's Menagerie; but this time it was not the only attraction. Booths and stalls had been set up and toys, sweets and balloons were on sale. There was a roundabout, a shooting-gallery, an Aunt Sally, a fortune-teller and a Punch-and-Judy show. A Fancy-Dress Parade was taking place. There were Sports and a Beauty Competition; and a piper was playing for Highland Dancing.

The air was full of noise and laughter. With

so many treats in store, how could anyone pass by? Maisie was getting ready to jump down even before the caravan came to a standstill. As for Grandpa, his old eyes were sparkling. "Drop anchor!" he cried, as excited as the others. "Macpherson, my boy, you'll be needing some funds this time. Can't go to a fair without spending."

"No thanks, Grandpa. I'll just use what's in my pocket and not spend any more," said Macpherson thriftily. "Come on, Maisie; I'll take you on the roundabouts."

"Oh yeth, pleathe, Macpherthon!"

They left Grandpa to tie up the pony and ran off to mingle with the crowds. As soon as the roundabout slowed down Maisie climbed on to a pink-and-white horse—very different from Slow-Coach—with Snowy still held firmly in her arms. "Look out!" called Macpherson, perching himself on a yellow ostrich. "We're off!"

The music blared out and away they went, up and down, round and round, faster and faster. Maisie shrieked with joy. Her hair-ribbon fluttered in the breeze. Her cheeks grew redder. The pink-and-white horse seemed to have wings. She could have stayed on for ever; but too soon the roundabout began to slow down.

Macpherson knew they could afford only one ride if they were to sample the other delights of the fair. He bought a balloon and some pink candy-floss for Maisie. He tried his luck at the shooting-gallery and received a toy duck for his pains. He knocked down Aunt Sally and won a coconut. With his last coin he took Maisie to see the Punch-and-Judy Show.

They were standing on tiptoe chuckling at the antics of the puppets when Grandpa joined them. There was a serious look on his face.

"What's up, Grandpa?"

"The money, Macpherson. It's not there. We've been robbed!"

"What? Oh Grandpa!"

Macpherson stared at him blankly. By now his own pockets were empty. If Grandpa's money was gone, they had not a penny between them. "How—how did it happen?"

The old man shook his head wearily. "Goodness knows! I had it hidden in a box at the back of the caravan. There's no sign of it. Maybe that burglar chap took it when we were camping last night."

"Oh Grandpa! What'll we do?"

Macpherson looked so downcast that the old man, always at his best in a crisis, put on a brighter face. "Not to worry, Macpherson my boy! We'll think of something. We've got enough food to last for ages. We'll manage!"

"Y-Yes, Grandpa!" Macpherson was not so sure.

Maisie, clutching her candy-floss, was away in a different world—Punch and Judy's world—but Macpherson had lost his taste for puppets. He was puzzling his brains. How could he earn some money to replace Grandpa's loss? It was all right to say they could manage, but all sorts of emergencies might happen. It would be difficult to continue their journey with empty pockets.

A sudden idea! The Sports were taking place in a nearby field. He would enter for one of the races and perhaps win a prize.

"Grandpa, I'm away to try my luck!"

He was off like a shot, scrambling over the fence. "Please sir, can I join in?" he asked.

"Why not? Everybody's welcome," said the man who was organising the Sports. "Would you like to try the sack race?"

"Yes, sir!"

Macpherson struggled into his sack, clutched it around him, tried a few practice steps—and fell flat on his face! Up again, he shuffled his way to the starting-point and joined the row of boys waiting for the "Ready! Steady! *Go!*"

They were off! The crowd began to shout and cheer. "Keep going, Macpherson! Pick yourself up!" He could hear Grandpa's voice above the others. He was down and up a dozen times, but at last he got the hang of it. Shuffle-shuffle; jump-jump; that was the way to do it. He was making progress. He was ahead of the rest. He could see the tape. One more jump. He had won!

"Ship ahoy! Well done, Macpherson!"

Macpherson scrambled out of the sack and waited for his prize. He hoped it might be money.

"Here you are, my boy. Congratulations!" The organiser shook hands with him and held out the prize.

"Th-Thanks very much, sir," said Macpherson, trying to hide his disappointment.

It was another coconut!

7

Macpherson in Trouble

"Come along, little girl. Why don't *you* enter?"

"What for?"

"The Junior Beauty Competition, my dear."

"What'th that?"

"Come along and find out," said the lady, taking Maisie by the hand. "What a pretty dress!"

"Yeth! Ithn't it?"

Macpherson, no richer except for a couple of coconuts and a toy duck, stood beside Grandpa watching the judges make their choice. It was not his idea of fun, looking at a lot of small girls parading in their best frocks. They all looked alike to Macpherson. The only difference was that one of them held a white kitten in her arms. Maisie was not going to be parted from Snowy after what had just happened.

"D'you know what, Macpherson! I think she's going to win," Grandpa whispered. "See! There's a chap getting ready to take her photograph—and someone else getting ready to place a crown on her head."

Miss Maisie Murphy—Junior Beauty Queen!

"Oh jings! Good for Maisie! I hope *she*'ll get a money prize."

His face fell when he saw the judges handing over an enormous box of chocolates tied up in red ribbon. Maisie had no fault to find with it. In her opinion it was far better than money.

"Look, Macpherthon! Thee what I've got!" She came running towards him, with her crown slipping over her brow. "Will I open it now or thave it for thupper?"

"Thave it," said Macpherson. "I mean, *save* it."

Grandpa laughed and bowed before the Queen. "Well done, Your Majesty! Open it now, if you like, Maisie, my dear." But Macpherson, feeling as if he were the only practical one of the trio, took the box from her.

"Give it to me, Maisie. I'll put it away safely in the caravan." He ran off and stowed it away along with his own prizes. Then suddenly the idea came into his head. He rushed back to join the others.

"Grandpa! I've got it!"

"What is it, my boy? Have you found the missing money?"

Macpherson shook his head. "No, but I know how to make some more! Slow-Coach!"

"What? Heave-ho, Macpherson! We can't sell *him*!"

"No, no, Grandpa! We can give rides on him. Tenpence a time on the piebald pony!"

The old man fingered his beard. "It's an

idea, Macpherson. Better ask permission first."

The organiser was all for it. "Why not?" said he. "It'll add to the fun. Go ahead!"

Macpherson went ahead! Slow-Coach, bored with being left alone, made no protest. He allowed himself to be led backwards and forwards, while the crowds of small boys and girls waited their turn.

"Come for a ride on the piebald pony! Ten-pence a time!" called Macpherson.

There was no lack of customers. The roundabouts were fun, but riding on a real pony was better. Grandpa took the money. Macpherson led Slow-Coach. Maisie trotted by his side, still wearing her crown.

At the end of the day they camped on the green near Pietro's lorry. Grandpa counted the money. "More than we had before! Well done, Macpherson! It was a great scheme. As long as we have Slow-Coach we needn't starve."

Then came the day when Macpherson was taken away by the police.

They were nearing the Border—the point where Scotland merged into England. The countryside grew wilder. There were fewer houses; more hills; many winding streams and ruined castles. Here, in the old days, bloodthirsty battles had been fought between the old enemies—the English and the Scots. Now everything was peaceful—until the policemen pounced on Macpherson and carried him off.

"What'th wrong? Where'th Macpherthon gone?" cried Maisie, clinging to Grandpa. The wild flowers fell unheeded from her hand and big tears began to trickle down her cheeks. She had changed into a jersey and skirt, and looked more like Maisie Murphy and less like a beauty queen. "Macpherthon! Come back!" she called—but the car, with the motor-cycle following, had already swooped out of sight.

"Well, that beats all!" said Grandpa. He looked suddenly older and frailer, as if, with Macpherson gone, all his life-blood had left him. Then, as Maisie's tears began to fall faster, he pulled himself up.

"Cheer up, Miss Murphy! This is an adventure! Let's go after him and solve the mystery."

Two in the caravan instead of three! Over the Border, clip-clop, clip-clop!

Macpherson was well ahead of them by now, sitting bolt upright beside the policeman. He was in England, but he took little notice of it. In any case, it seemed just the same as Scotland—rolling hills, winding streams, ruined castles. How could he enjoy looking at scenery, with Grandpa and Maisie left behind?

He tried to talk to the policeman but the man would not listen. His mind seemed to be taken up with his driving. They were travelling at such a speed that the motor-cycle could scarcely keep up with them. Round corners with the siren blowing! Up steep hills as if they were flying! Into a small town, scattering the people right and left!

They drew up at the police station in the middle of the street.

"Come along, my lad! In here!" said the policeman.

Macpherson was bundled into a small room where a stern-faced man addressed him. "What's this you've been up to? How did a young chap like you come to be in possession of stolen goods?"

"Please, sir, I don't know, sir. It's all a mistake."

The stern-faced man opened out the parcel. No mistake! A heap of jewellery tumbled out on to the table. "Lady Rutherford's jewels! We've been on the trail of that lot for ages! How did you get hold of them? Come on; speak up!"

"I didn't steal them! I'm not a burglar,"

protested Macpherson. Then suddenly he re-membered. The burglar! The one he and Battling Jimmy Smith had caught. It must have been him!

Macpherson blurted out his story while the policemen listened with no expression on their faces. They had heard too many stories in their day to believe anything without evidence. They had heard of Battling Jimmy Smith and knew the village in which he lived, so they were half-inclined to think Macpherson was telling the truth. What they wanted was proof.

"What was the name of the policeman?"

"Please, sir, I'm not sure. I think it was Brown."

The men looked at each other. "It could have been Bill Brown. Hold on! We can ring up and find out."

Macpherson stood uneasily on one foot while the call was put through, but he soon relaxed when he realised that his story was being confirmed.

"Right! Well, that's that! I'm glad to hear the lad's in the clear. Yes! I'll pass on the good news." The stern-faced man put down the receiver and turned to Macpherson. Even with good news to tell, he still looked stern. "There's a reward waiting for you, my lad. Five hundred pounds. They've put it in the bank for you."

"Five hundred pounds!" Macpherson gaped at him. He was a millionaire! He had a bank balance to his name! He could go in through the great doorway of the Bank of Scotland and find the manager bowing to him.

"*Good* morning, Mr Macpherson, sir! A pleasure to see you! What can we do for you today? Would you like some money out of your account? A bagful of silver? Certainly, Mr Macpherson, sir! Only too pleased! Would you kindly step this way . . . ?"

"Here! Take this!"

A cup of tea was thrust into the boy's hand. Though the men still spoke to him in gruff voices, they were trying their best to be friendly. All the same, even though he was a millionaire, Macpherson still had a big worry on his mind.

"What about Grandpa and the caravan? I'll have to get back to him. He'll wonder what's happened."

The Scottish policeman rose to his feet. "Okay, young fellow! You can have a ride on the back of my bike. I'll have to be on my way home. We'll soon meet them on the road." He looked down at Macpherson, sipping his tea.

"I must say, for a chap your size, you seem to have your fill of adventures."

"Yes, so I do!" agreed Macpherson, grinning at him.

It was exciting, swooping back towards the Border on the policeman's motor-cycle. Macpherson had to cling on, while the wind ruffled his hair and blew a bright colour into his cheeks. All he could see was the man's broad back in front of him. Then suddenly the cycle swerved to the side and came to a standstill.

"Caravan ahead! This is where we part. Cheerio, lad, and the best of luck."

The motor-cycle roared away leaving Macpherson by the roadside gazing at Slow-Coach coming clip-clopping towards him.

"Ship ahoy!" called Grandpa. "What's the score, Macpherson?"

"All square! D'you know what, Grandpa!— We're millionaires!"

It was wonderful to be back in the caravan telling the tale to Grandpa and Maisie, and deciding how to spend the money when he got home. By the time they had travelled another mile, Macpherson had bought a helicopter for himself, a ship for Grandpa, a washing machine for Aunt Janet, and a sweet shop for

Maisie full of lollipops and chocolate creams.

It was exciting, too, to be in a new country. Now that he could look about him, Macpherson began to notice the difference. The roads were wider; the countryside less bare. There were more villages and small towns; and, when he stopped to buy food, the people talked to him in a different accent.

"I had to say it *three* times," he told Grandpa, as he scrambled back into the caravan with his purchases. "The baker couldn't understand me when I asked for scones. He called them *scoans*."

"As long as they taste like scones, that's all right!" said Grandpa. "How's the appetite, Macpherson? Ready for another meal?"

"Ay, ay, sir! Ready and willing!"

"Yeth; tho am I!"

The fresh air had sharpened all their appetites, including the pony's. Slow-Coach would eat anything from left-over scones to coconut-shells. Whenever a fresh patch of grass by the roadside took his fancy, he would draw up and help himself. "All the same, he's worth feeding," said Grandpa, letting him take his time. "Don't forget, he's our bread-winner if we run short of ready money; and, anyway, there's no hurry."

That was the best of it. No hurry! No cross grocer shouting, "Macpherson! Where's that good-for-nothing message-boy? Hurry up, or I'll skin you alive!"

They were dawdling along a country lane when Macpherson suddenly called out: "Look, Grandpa! A hitch-hiker! He's wearing a kilt! He must come from Scotland! Let's stop and give him a lift."

The man was limping along the dusty road, with a dog—as weary-looking as himself—at his heels. As they drew up, they saw that the man in the kilt looked thin and ill. The dog, too, seemed scarcely able to drag himself along.

"Hi there! Where are you going? Would you like a lift?"

At the sound of a friendly Scots voice the man looked up. For a moment his face brightened. Then he staggered and fell down in a crumpled heap on the roadside. The dog stood over him, licking his pale face and whining pathetically.

"Oh dear! Ith he dead?" asked Maisie, trembling with alarm.

"Fainted, more likely," said Grandpa, getting down as fast as he could. "The poor soul's starving, by the look of him. Get some food ready, Macpherson."

For the next few moments they were all too busy to speak. Macpherson got out the stove and lit it, ready to boil the kettle. Maisie found some milk which she poured into a saucer for the starving dog. The animal lapped up a little of it, then went back to stand by the figure lying on the ground. Hungry though the dog was, he would not feed himself while his master lay ill.

Grandpa tried to prop the man up in his arms. A faint trace of colour was coming back to his face, and he was trying to mumble some words.

"Take it easy," said Grandpa quietly. "You'll soon be all right. What you need is something to eat."

"Sorry to trouble you," muttered the man. "I'm down on my luck. . . ."

"It's no trouble," Grandpa assured him. "We're glad to meet someone from Scotland. As to being down on your luck, we've been in the same state ourselves. Is that tea ready, Macpherson?"

"Ay, ay, sir! Coming up!"

Macpherson made the tea strong and sweet. As the man sipped it, every mouthful seemed to revive him. The dog, too, seeing his master settled, went back to the saucer of milk and drank up every drop. Meantime, Macpherson buttered some scones and brought out eggs and bacon from the caravan.

While the meal was being prepared Grandpa studied the man in the shabby kilt. He looked young—little more than a boy—though his face was so strained and weary. He seemed underfed and footsore, as if he had tramped many long miles. His coat was threadbare and the soles of his shoes worn through. Small wonder that he had been limping! Yet, as he began to recover, there was a proud air about him, as if he could conquer the world if he tried.

He spoke with dignity when he thanked

Grandpa. "I'd better push on," he said, trying to get to his feet and calling the dog to him. "You've been very kind to me, sir. Come, Rory!"

The dog came forward, ready to move off at his master's command; but Grandpa would not hear of them going. "Nonsense! Stay and share our meal. You're not fit for the road yet. Tell me, where have you come from, and what's your name?"

"My name? Dugald McLeod from the island of Skye." The proud look came into his eye as he spoke of his native country. "It is a beautiful place, but I could get no work there."

"What kind of work are you looking for?"

"Anything! Gardening, maybe. We've tramped all over—Rory and me—without any luck. Now my money's run out...." He passed his hand wearily across his brow.

"Never mind, lad! Maybe your luck's going to turn," said Grandpa in a cheerful voice. "No more questions till you've fed." He sniffed the air. "That's a fine tasty smell, Macpherson! Dish it up!"

There was little conversation during the meal. It was obvious that this was the first time Dugald—or the dog—had eaten for days. Maisie trotted backwards and forwards to the caravan, bringing out every item of food she could find—even lollipops. At last, Dugald gave a satisfied sigh. "No more! I couldn't eat another bite!"

The dog stretched out beside him and fell into a satisfied sleep. His master, too, began to drowse, while Grandpa put the kettle back on the stove.

"Better get your feet bathed, lad, and then we'll give you a lift along the road. Maybe Macpherson'll walk for a bit."

"Tho will I," offered Maisie. "I can carry Thnowy and let the wee dog have a ride."

By the time they were packed up and ready to go Dugald had told them more about his life on the island of Skye and of his long trudge in search of work.

"I want to go back some day and buy a farm; but I must make some money first."

Macpherson thought of his five hundred pounds. Would that be enough to buy a farm? But perhaps Dugald with his proud air, would prefer to earn his own money.

"Can you play the pipes?" Macpherson asked him.

"Indeed I can! Maybe if I had brought them with me I could have earned some money," said Dugald. A look of despair came into his eyes. "It seems hopeless. I wonder if I should turn back . . . ?"

"No!" said Grandpa firmly. "No turning back! Once you've set your mind on something, carry straight on. Come along, lad! Into the caravan!"

It was easy enough for Macpherson to keep pace with Slow-Coach, but Maisie wanted to stop to pick the wild flowers from the hedge-rows. Macpherson tried to urge her on. "Hurry up, you! You'll be left behind!"

"I'm hurry-up-ing!" said Maisie breathlessly. She picked a last wild rose from the hedge, then called out: "Oh look, Macpher-thon! I can thee a Red Indian in the field."

"Nonsense!" said Macpherson crossly. "Don't tell tarradiddles!"

"It'th true! Ever tho many Red Indianth and ever tho many cowboyth. . . ."

In spite of himself, Macpherson went to look. "Mercy me!" he gasped, staring in amazement. "It's a Wild West film!"

8

Macpherson, Film-Star

"Stop, Grandpa! Stop!"

Macpherson was running breathlessly after the caravan, which was turning a corner ahead of him.

"Ahoy, Macpherson! What's up?" called Grandpa, tugging at the reins.

"Oh Grandpa! Isn't it exciting? They're making a film in that field over there. Let's go and watch. Red Indians and cowboys!"

"Shiver me timbers! That's too good to miss!" said the old man, drawing in to the side of the road. "Drop anchor! Do you want to stay in the caravan and rest, Dugald, or would you like to come with us?"

"I'll come!" Dugald was already scrambling down, as excited as Macpherson. "Cowboys and Indians! They're my favourites!"

He helped to tether Slow-Coach to the fence. Then they all scrambled over into the field— the dog and kitten, too. Maisie's eyes almost popped out of her head at the sights she saw.

The field was crowded with colourful characters, dressed up for their parts, with stained faces and feathered head-gear. Some were on horseback; others were testing guns and tomahawks and lassoes; and the director was shouting his orders through a megaphone.

"Into your places, everybody! Get lined up! We'll soon be ready to shoot."

Maisie began to tremble. "Did you hear that? He'th going to kill them all!"

"Of course he isn't, silly! He's going to film them," said Macpherson in his know-all voice. "Oh look, there's a covered wagon. It looks just the same as our caravan...."

Just then the director caught sight of them and waved them forward. "Fine!" said he, looking them up and down. "You'll fit in all right. Who sent you?" Without waiting for a reply, he went on: "We can use the lot of you, especially the boy. What's your name? Never mind! Come this way!"

It all happened so quickly that there was no chance to explain. Before they could protest, they were drawn into the thick of the throng. Maisie was whisked away into a tent to be dressed up. Someone began to slap paint on Grandpa's face and stick feathers in his hair. Everyone crowded round to admire Dugald's kilt and wonder how it would fit into a Wild West picture.

"Can you ride a horse?" the director asked Macpherson; and, as usual, he gave him no time to reply. "Right! You'd better be a cowboy. Change your clothes as quickly as you can. Mustn't keep the cameras waiting ..."

Macpherson was sure that he was dreaming; but, if so, what a wonderful dream! He pulled off his shabby green jersey and put on the cowboy suit. Then he joined the queue to be made up.

When he came out of the tent he was so transformed that Maisie could not recognise him.

"Where'th Macpherthon?" she asked. "I've lotht him."

"I'm here!" said Macpherson. "Who are you supposed to be?"

"I'm Maithie Murphy—I think," she said in a puzzled voice. "Oh Macpherthon! It'th you! You look different!"

Maisie looked different herself. Her skin was brown. She was barefoot and dressed in a long ragged gown. She would rather have changed into her velvet dress so that she could look her best, but this was no time for beauty queens.

"You're supposed to be running away from

the Indians," shouted the man with the megaphone. "Stand over there and get ready for action."

Maisie, tripping over her dress, went to join the others, and stared up at a tall Indian with a straggly beard.

"Heave-ho, my hearty!" he called out in a familiar voice.

"Merthy! It'th Grandpa! You don't look like yourthelf! You're awful funny!" she giggled.

The strangest of all was Dugald in his kilt. The director was determined to use the young Scot just as he was, whether he fitted into the picture or not. "It'll make a fine splash of colour, that skirt."

"Skirt!" said Dugald in a hurt voice. "It's a kilt! The McLeod tartan. . . ."

"Okay! Okay! Never mind what it's called. Just stand over there. You can keep the dog at your heel, if you like."

"Can I have Thnowy?" asked Maisie; but no one was listening. In any case, the kitten was too frightened to come any nearer than the hedgerow. She sat there watching the scene and giving a bewildered *miaow* now and then. It was all too much for a small kitten. Indeed, it was almost too much for Maisie. Her hero,

Macpherson, was being taken away from her, and she was left with strangers, each one looking fiercer and more warlike than the next.

"Haven't you got a horse yet?" shouted the director, looking at Macpherson. "Find one, for goodness' sake!"

At that moment, as if hearing his cue, Slow-Coach poked his head over the fence and gave a loud neigh.

"He'll do! Can we borrow him and the caravan, too? Right! Get busy! Bring him into the field! Quickly now! Must start shooting . . . ."

For the next hour or so they all lived in a dream. There was so much noise and confusion, so much whooping and shouting, that it was difficult to tell what they were all supposed to be doing. At one time the Red Indians were chasing the cowboys. The next moment the order was reversed. The cowboys began chasing the Indians! No one knew who was winning.

The field had become a prairie. Guns were fired; tomahawks flew through the air; lassoes were whirling in every direction. The director shouted his orders; the cameras whirred; the covered wagons rattled and creaked across the crowded field.

Macpherson, seated on Slow-Coach's broad

back, was in his element. "That young fella's the best actor of the lot," said the man with the megaphone. But Macpherson was not acting. He was enjoying himself! He had forgotten about the cameras and the film. This was fun!

"Whoopee! Get a move on, Slow-Coach! The Indians are after us! Oh my! I wonder what Old Skinflint would say if he could see me now!"

It did not occur to Macpherson that, months later, Old Skinflint could see him as he was now, riding the range on a piebald pony. That is, if the tight-fisted grocer would spend his money on a seat in the local cinema. He would see Grandpa, too, a dignified old Indian, calmly smoking his pipe while the battle raged around him. He would see a small barefoot girl tripping over her dress and sitting down with a bump while a tomahawk missed her by inches. He would see a kilted figure with a dog at his heels, fighting his way into the midst of the battle.

It was unlikely that Old Skinflint would ever go to the cinema; but Miss Peacock and Mr Grim would go. Perhaps even Aunt Janet, if she was coaxed. The day would come when Macpherson and Grandpa and Maisie would sit side-by-side on plush seats, watching themselves on the screen.

Maisie, of course, would be sucking a lollipop. "Oh look, there'th Macpherthon! Merthy! Ith that Grandpa? Who'th that? Oh, it'th me!"

That was far away in the future. The present was exciting enough; so exciting that Macpherson was surprised to hear the director shout: "Cut! We've done a good day's work. All you extras can line up now and get paid...."

Paid! Macpherson had not realised that he and the others were earning money while they were enjoying themselves. Real money! Even Maisie's small fists were full of notes when she went to pick up Snowy from the sideline. When they counted it all up, they realised they were richer than they had ever been before—and all because they had been playing a game of Cowboys and Indians!

"Hi you; young fella!" The director called out to Macpherson. "If ever you want a job get in touch with my studios. I might make something of you."

"Yes, sir; thank you, sir,"—but how could Macpherson be a film-star when there were so many other things he wanted to be? Inventor; explorer; detective; footballer; Prime Minister; Lord Provost of Glasgow. He would need a hundred lives.

It was difficult to come down to earth. They had changed back into their everyday clothes, but their faces were still streaked with make-up. Their minds were still full of the Wild West, and they could talk of nothing else as they got ready to move off in the caravan.

This time Dugald insisted on walking, with Rory at his heels. "I'm feeling fine now," he said to Grandpa, holding himself up proudly. "I'd like you to take some of my money to pay for the help you gave me."

"Nonsense, lad! It'll be a good nest-egg for you, to start you off. I told you your luck would turn! Heave-ho, my hearties! Let's be off!"

They were all talking so much about the adventures of the day that they did not notice the black clouds gathering in the sky. A large plop of rain landed on Maisie's nose.

"Merthy! It'th wet!"

Maisie had forgotten about rain. In Glasgow she was often soaked to the skin. It was all part of the rough-and-tumble life she led. But this had been such a sunny holiday that the sudden downpour took them all by surprise.

"Rain! Rain! Go to Spain," sang out Grandpa, as the clouds opened and a torrent, like a waterfall, tumbled down from the sky. "Under cover, everybody! Get out the tarpaulins!"

They drew in to the side of the road and took what shelter they could find. Maisie was hoisted into the back of the caravan, where she kept Snowy warm and dry. The dog leapt up beside her, while the others huddled under a waterproof cover. They flung another over Slow-Coach who stood stamping his clumsy feet in the puddles and twitching his tail in disgust. It was obvious that he, too, hated the downpour.

As the drenching rain lashed down on them, they began to look more and more bedraggled. Their make-up trickled down their cheeks as the raindrops drove into their faces.

"We're a queer-looking lot," grinned Grandpa. "It's a blessing there's no one to see us!"

But there *was* someone!

He came striding along the road, looking as down on his luck as Dugald had been. His coat was in tatters. His ancient plus-fours were shapeless and threadbare. He wore a pair of old boots on his feet and a battered hat on his head. His weather-beaten face was almost hidden by a fierce moustache; and he had a pair of piercing eyes through which he gazed at the company by the roadside.

"Care to join us, chum?" said Grandpa, making room under the tarpaulin. "We can give you something to eat once the rain goes off. It's no fun being homeless in weather like this."

The man's eyebrows shot up and down. "Homeless!" he boomed. "My dear man, what are you talking about? Look over there!"

Grandpa could see nothing over there except driving rain; but Macpherson's eyes were sharper. "It's a great big house, like a castle."

"It *is* a castle," said the man, shaking the raindrops off his battered hat. "That's where I live."

"What?" Macpherson stared at the ragged

coat and down-at-heel boots. "You're—you're not a Lord, are you?"

"No! I'm a Duke!"

"Goodness gracious me!"

Macpherson was flabbergasted. The only Dukes he had seen were in photographs, and *they* were dressed for the part. They wore velvet cloaks edged with ermine. They had coronets on their heads. They rode about in golden coaches. He had never imagined that a real Duke could look like a scarecrow.

"We're only human beings, you know!" said the Duke, guessing his thoughts. He accepted Grandpa's offer of shelter, and shot an amused glance at Macpherson. "I like the simple life, as you do, by the look of you. For all I know, you might be a Prince."

"Me? I'm just a message-boy!" said Macpherson, as he rubbed some of the make-up off his face. "Well, actually, I was a cowboy a short time ago. . . ."

The Duke heard the whole story as he huddled beside them under the waterproof sheet. He seemed pleased with their adventures. "Go on, boy! Tell me some more! What happened next?"

"Macpherthon!" Maisie's piping voice interrupted them from the back of the caravan.

"It'th thtopped raining."

"So it has," said the Duke, rising and shaking his wet clothes. "If you have no other pressing engagements, may I have the pleasure of your company tonight?"

"At the castle?" gasped Macpherson.

"Where else? There are plenty of outhouses where you can stay the night, if you like; and you must all come and have dinner with me. Eight o'clock! Sharp!"

9

The Last Lap

At eight o'clock sharp they rang the great bell at the castle door.

Maisie was dressed up in her velvet frock and patent-leather shoes. Macpherson had changed into a clean jersey. Grandpa had trimmed his beard. Dugald had pressed his kilt and tried to put a shine on his shabby shoes. They had all done their best in one way or another, to spruce themselves up.

Even so, they looked an odd group to be standing on the doorstep of such a stately home. Especially when they saw the dignified figure who had come to open the door.

"Ith he a Duke, too?" asked Maisie, in an awed whisper.

"No, of course not, silly! He's the butler!" Macpherson gave her a push forward. "Mind your manners!"

The butler marched ahead of them with stately steps, and ushered them into a large room where their host was waiting. They had a glimpse of family portraits on the wall. They could see priceless ornaments in the room. They saw rich carpets and curtains; but the most surprising sight was the Duke himself.

"Aha! So we've all got ourselves dressed up, I see!" he said, coming forward to meet them. He twitched his eyebrows at Macpherson. "Do I look more like a Duke now?"

"Oh yes, Your Grace, sir!"

All the same, Macpherson was a trifle disappointed that the Duke was not wearing his coronet. He had put on a jacket of rich ruby velvet. He wore knee-breeches and shoes with silver buckles. There was certainly nothing of the scarecrow about him now. He looked as if he had been polished and scrubbed until even his moustache shone like silk.

"Come along! Let's eat! I hope you're hungry?"

"Yeth! We're thtarving!" said Maisie.

What a change from picnicking by the wayside! The dining-room table was so big that they all seemed to be miles away from each other. A footman stood behind the Duke, while servants dressed in livery carried round silver dishes to set before the guests. They had never before seen such an array of spoons and knives and forks.

At first they were all too tongue-tied to speak. Except Maisie!

"What'th thith?" she asked, peering into one of the silver dishes.

Macpherson would have kicked her on the shins had he not been so far away; but the Duke did not seem to mind her questions.

"It's a partridge, my dear. I hope you'll like it."

"Ith it all for me?"

"Yes! You can have more, if you like."

"Merthy me!"

There were so many courses that they lost count. There was soup and fish and game and ham, and an enormous iced pudding in the shape of the Duke's castle. There was fruit to finish off with—big bunches of grapes from His Grace's greenhouse.

"I must show you round the gardens in the morning," said he, lighting a cigar. "I have acres and acres of ground. The trouble is, I can't get enough help."

Macpherson sat up suddenly and looked across at Dugald whose face was flushed with excitement. "Please, Your Grace, sir; *he*'s looking for a job. . . ."

It was all settled before the coffee was served in tiny gold cups. Dugald was to stay in one of the cottages and help in the Duke's garden.

"They will be pleased to learn about my good fortune back home in the island of Skye," he said, sitting up straight. "This has been the luckiest day of my life."

It had been a lucky—and long—day for them all. Especially for someone as young, and as full of food, as Maisie. Try as she would, she could no longer keep her eyes open.

"Mithter Duke," she said in a far-away voice. "I'm ever tho thleepy...."

With that, she disgraced herself in Macpherson's sight by laying her head down on the polished table and falling fast asleep. No amount of pushing or prodding would waken her. Maisie was out for the count.

The Duke turned to the footman behind his chair and said, "Find Mrs Maxwell. Ask her to get a room ready for Miss Murphy."

He smiled at his guests. "Don't worry! My housekeeper will see to everything. The poor child's worn out. She had better stay here for the night. Come and fetch her in the morning." He rose from the table. "What we all need is a good night's rest."

Macpherson slept soundly in the little stable-loft, with Slow-Coach stamping his feet down below. In the morning, he woke bright and early. Before the others were stirring, he ran out to explore the grounds. The air was crisp and fresh, filled with the perfume of roses. The gardens and lawns stretched far away down to a lake where dozens of swans and ducks were floating on the water.

"Lucky Dugald!" thought Macpherson, filling his lungs with the scented air. How wonderful to work here rather than in a dingy grocer's shop! Yet, he would miss Glasgow; it was a great place....

A voice called out to him. "Good-morning to you! *You*'re out bright and early!" It was the Duke dressed once more in his shabby clothes. He carried a spade. "I'm off to do some digging in the kitchen-garden. Must keep on the move! Don't like to be idle!"

Macpherson offered to help. "No thanks, my boy! I like doing it myself. All the same, I'll be glad when that fellow Dugald settles in. Can't cope with it *all* on my own. As for you, you'd better waken up Miss Murphy and have your breakfast. I dare say you're feeling peckish."

Macpherson hurried up to the front door and rang the bell.

"Well, what do *you* want?" said the butler, in his most pompous voice.

"Please, sir, I'm—er—looking for Miss

M-Maisie M-Murphy." No wonder Macpherson stammered! The butler was far more terrifying than the Duke.

The man looked down at Macpherson from his lofty height. There was a pained note in his voice when he spoke. "Wait there and I'll fetch Mrs Maxwell." Macpherson felt that he was being a nuisance.

"The Duke told me to ask," he said, trying to justify himself. "I'm s-sorry to t-trouble you...."

"No trouble," said the butler in a voice that meant the opposite. "Mrs Maxwell! Would you attend to this young—er—gentleman?"

The housekeeper came bustling forward, plump and smiling. "This way, my boy!" She led him up a wide staircase and into the biggest bedroom he had ever seen. "Here she is! Waken her up and I'll see about breakfast!"

Maisie lay fast asleep in a four-poster bed, looking like a very small pea in a very large pod.

"Hi, you! Waken up!" Macpherson shook her gently by the shoulders.

Maisie sighed and opened her eyes. She looked up at the great canopy overhead. "Where am I? Where'th Macpherthon?"

"I'm here, silly!"

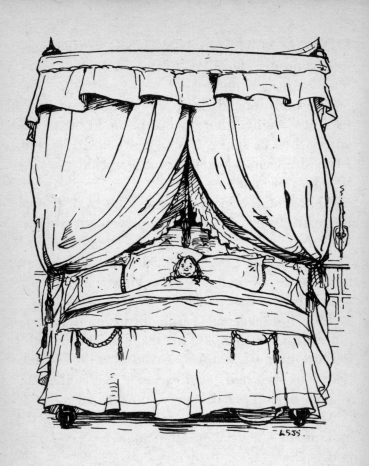

"Oh well, that'th all right!"

Maisie sat up, not caring whether she was in a palace or a prison. "What'th happening?"

As if in answer to her question the door opened and in came a footman bearing a large silver tray.

"Breakfast for two, sir," he said, setting it on a table beside the bed.

Maisie, who had eaten so much the night before, was now starving. So was Macpherson. He did justice to the bacon and eggs and sausages and hot rolls and thin slices of toast with marmalade. Maisie sipped her tea from a delicate china cup, then gave a blissful sigh. "Thith ith great, Macpherthon! I think I'll thtay here!"

"Okay!" said Macpherson, finishing off the toast, "We'll go back to Glasgow without you."

Maisie sat bolt upright. "No, you'll not. Ith it all over, Macpherthon? Have we got to go home?"

Macpherson nodded. To cheer himself up—as well as Maisie—he tried to remember all the good things about Glasgow. "There's the River Clyde, and the big shops, and the parks, and the Highland bobby, and the Bank of Scotland with five hundred pounds in it. . . ."

"And the twinth!" Maisie suddenly remembered Him and Her. "Oh Macpherthon! I wonder if the new baby'th come?" She scrambled out of bed in a hurry. "Come on! Let'th go home!"

It was over! Yet not all over.

There was still the journey home, filled with so many happenings that they lost count.

There was the day when Maisie tumbled out of the back of the caravan, and was not missed till she had been left behind for miles.

There was the day when they camped on the seashore and went in to swim—even Slow-Coach—without noticing that they were being cut off by the tide.

There was the most exciting day of all, the day they helped to round up Tarzan who had escaped from Mistress Mackay's Menagerie.

There was the day the wheel came off the caravan; the day they met the gypsies and shared their camp fire; the day when Slow-Coach stumbled over a fallen tree trunk and landed them all in the ditch.

And then there was the day when Grandpa took firm hold of the reins and called out: "Ship ahoy, my hearties! Full steam ahead! Land in sight!"

They were back in the streets of Glasgow!

Everything was the same—the streets; the River Clyde; the shops; the skyscrapers; the Highland bobby.

"Welcome home! Man, Macpherson, Glasgow's been the quiet place without you!"

Nothing had changed—except themselves.

Maisie's face was chubbier and rosier. Grandpa looked younger and livelier. Macpherson was as brown as a berry.

Slow-Coach put on a final spurt as they neared the Tenements.

"Oh look, Grandpa! There's Aunt Janet at the window. Mercy me! She's waving! She looks quite pleased to see us back." Macpherson grinned up at the old man. "Hasn't it been fun, Grandpa, but isn't it great to be coming home? After all, we can still have adventures in Glasgow."

More stories about MACPHERSON by Lavinia Derwent, also published by Knight Books:

MACPHERSON'S SKYSCRAPER

One morning, when Macpherson arrived for work at McGlashan's grocery, he was astonished to find the shop ransacked by burglars. Macpherson is used to surprises but then came a far greater shock – the news that his home was to be pulled down . . .

MACPHERSON'S LIGHTHOUSE ADVENTURE

Macpherson is off for a fortnight's free holiday at the seaside, where there is no shortage of surprises for the young errand boy. But most exciting of all is his adventure at the lighthouse . . .

MACPHERSON'S ISLAND

Grandpa is ill and needs a holiday to recover, but Macpherson can see no way of arranging this. Then, unexpectedly, his luck changes and soon he is off with Grandpa and Maisie Murphy to stay in a haunted castle on Seagull Island!

KNIGHT BOOKS